"Passion

"I liked Tony the minute .... even better. When I was president of the Western Division of Dickson
Media, our office printed Tony's newspaper, and I was usually
the first person to read his weekly columns. I recognized the
passion and compassion of his writing. He continues to make me
laugh, inspire me and remind me of the great beauty of the people and the land of the great plains."

Bill Derby, publisher
The News and Neighbor
Johnson City, TN

He gets inside the mirror

"It's been said that journalists provide a mirror of life. Tony
Bender changed that rule by paying not so much attention to
what's in the mirror as what's inside it. His subjects du'jour
range from side-splitting humor to tear-inducing drama. What
does his effort produce? Sometimes funny, sometimes provoca-
tive, sometimes poignant but always enjoyable reading."

Roger Bailey, executive director
North Dakota Newspaper Association

"You'll laugh..."

"Tony Bender is funny. Tony Bender's books are funny. Believe
me, you'll laugh when you read this book... You'll laugh and
sometimes you'll feel inspired. The guy's that good."

Mike Jacobs, editor
Grand Forks Herald

"A rare gift"

"Tony Bender has a rare gift for observing and chronicling the feats and foibles of real people and real life. Shades of Hemingway's quiet strength and Kerouac's satiric edge. But most of all, *The Great and Mighty Da-Da* is pure Bender."

Bob Booker, Jones Radio Network, Denver, Co

"Bender has been embraced"

"The people of the plains are not easily impressed. They scoff at east coast puffery, wrinkle noses at west coast trendism. They are a common sense, no-nonsense lot with a work ethic unequaled in America. They do not embrace easily writers, philosophers or humorists. Yet Tony Bender has been embraced out here on the prairie. For in his writing, on pages turned by tired, callused hands, the people of the high plains recognize themselves.

He is in their face, at their side, jabbing, poking, tickling, kicking butt, consoling and always understanding. For more than a decade, Bender's readers have laughed with him and shed secret tears when no one can see behind the pages of a score of small weekly newspapers and medium size dailies in the Dakotas. He has been their loosely-kept secret. They have clipped the columns, and they yellow in scrap books, adorn refrigerators or are mailed off to exotic locales where ex-patriots still yearn for the elbow room and buffalo grass.

'He is in their face, at their side, jabbing, poking, tickling, kicking butt, consoling and always understanding.'

In 2000, with the publication of his first collection, *Loons in the Kitchen*, the secret was completely out. New readers raved and bought extra copies, so they could share this powerful voice from the plains who describes unerringly the hard-scrabble farmers and bigger-than-life small-town personalities. Long time readers smiled smugly at the fuss, for he is one of their own. Now Bender is back, his voice growing ever clearer, his vision sharper, his punctuation consistently abysmal. But book editors must have work. With *The Great and Mighty Da-Da*, Bender returns with new missives, unique insights and common sense philosophies. Bender is back. Well, the truth is, he never really went away."—*Allan Burke, Emmons County Record, Linton, ND*

REDHEAD

PUBLISHING, INC.

The Great and Mighty Da-Da

by Tony Bender

Cover photography by Sherry Slycord

Cover design by Redhead Publishing

Edited by Jane Haas

The Great and Mighty Da-Da

International Standard Book Number: 0-9705442-1-9

Published by:

Redhead Publishing
119 West Main Street
Ashley, ND 58413

1-701-288-3531

redhead@drtel.net
www.ashleynd.com
www.wisheknd.com
www.tonybender.com

Printed in the United States of America

Foreword

Here we are again. I hadn't planned to be back in this place with a second collection of stories, certainly not so soon, but it really wasn't my doing.

After my first collection, *Loons in the Kitchen*, came out, I announced the collection to a circle of family, friends, readers and acquaintances.

"Does it have this one...?" they would ask. "I hope you included..." And they would list a personal favorite. Almost always the answer was no. As I traveled, longtime readers of my column would meet me at book signings and comment on a particular favorite, and usually, it wasn't one I had included in the first book.

It is hard as a writer to measure your own work. Sometimes the result is immediately clear. Other times, years removed from the moment, when you are more objective, you can much more easily see the flaws and on rarer occasions, excellence. If not excellence, then at least the knowledge that it was the best you could do at the time. It seems to me that some days, some pieces just *read better* than on others. Perhaps it has something to do with the alignment of planets or barometric pressure. I don't know. In the end, it is the reader who makes the judgement.

Some of the readers' favorites, in my judgement, were pieces in which the thought and sentiment of the column was pure, the writing almost sinful. So, on some of them, I did tweak a bit here and there. *Benches*, a longtime reader favorite, was agonizingly revised. Such a revision was hard. I wanted to remain true to the writer I was a decade ago, but my voice is clearer now, most days, and because the story was close to my heart, I wanted it told as best I could.

There are two groups of writers. Those who would publish every word they have ever committed to paper. And those who would never publish a word because they are not perfect. The first group is comprised of the insane and the gifted. I mostly am hunkered down with the second group, with brief visitations to the first.

Giving so many others a say in the compilation of *The Great and Mighty Da-Da* wasn't easy, but when I looked at the pieces they had favored, I allowed that perhaps they were right.

You can never trust a writer to tell you what is good. Every one of us will look you in the eye and tell you we have written a masterpiece. And almost always we are lying.

Writing a personal column is a curious exercise with a great deal of presumption involved. Presumption that your life or your view of life is special. On my best days, I find I am not really writing about myself. I am writing about you, your children and your lives. Columns are read and you say, "That is me!"

A personal column writer floats his pieces out each week and many times nothing floats back. Other times, after folks have struck up a conversation in the line at the DMV, at the grocery store, and they find out who you are, they will name a favorite column.

We are needy souls, writers, and we never fail to caress a compliment and remember it. Thus, this book was born.

I chose the title of this book, *The Great and Mighty Da-Da*, because it reflects what I view as my most important job. I am a writer. A publisher. But most importantly, I am a husband and a father. Sometimes the writer in me jealously guards his time. But I am learning to heed the calls from my family. I have realized that I must live in order to write. Who would want to read the rantings of some wizened old hermit, locked away in a corner? Writing isn't that hard. It just requires honesty. Honesty. Wrenching, soul-searching, embarrassing honesty—now that's the hard part! Writing should come from the heart. If you can accomplish that, I think you'll get along just fine.

There are some new pieces in this book that have a place in my heart because that is where they were born. *The House David Built, What Friends Will Do, Dad Hugged Me, Ryan's Hope,* and *Getting By* are among the essays which allowed me a rare measure of satisfaction with the story told. The reader must be satisfied first and foremost. But the writer must be satisfied as well, or his dissatisfaction is reflected in the work.

The last line in the *Loons* foreword reads, "Now it is time to move on." Well, I was wrong. My readers demanded I walk those paths of the past one more time.

That I get it right this time.

I enjoyed the journey.

Now it is time to move on.

I mean it this time.

—Tony Bender

Dedication

Norman Bender
1938-1993

Benjamin Bender
1910-1995

John Spilloway
1911-1995

Great and Mighty Da-Das all.

Table of Contents

POLITICS AS UNUSUAL

TECHNOLOGY ISSUES

INK IN MY VEINS

FAMILY WAYS

SEASONS

RESOLVE

Out Here on the Prairie

Mothers are the poets of the universe.

Tony Bender
Oh Brothers, 1993

Ryan's Hope

The difference is the vent windows. That's how you tell them apart. That's how you know if you're looking at a 1967 Camaro. Or a sixty-eight.

That first year they had vents, so on a blistering hot summer day, you could crank them wide open and feel the rush of air whipping by your grin at 90 mph.

Mike Carlsen sneers at sixty-eights. They are pretenders. But if his upper lip curls at a '68, it snarls at the mention of a Honda Prelude.

The Camaro was freedom. Youth. Laughs. Heads pasted back in second gear, tires smoking.

The Honda was button-down collars. Responsibility. Great gas mileage.

"Stupidity." That was the reason.

That is the only explanation Mike has for trading that '67 Camaro in on that Honda Prelude. The salesman drooled. And the '67 with the vent windows did not last a day on the lot before it was snatched up by a wiser man.

There had been pressure. Time to grow up, folks said. Time to cast off childish things. Trade the blue jeans in for polyester slacks. Get from behind the wheel and get behind the desk. Abandon the 327 for the 9 to 5.

That is what they told him.

And Mike listened.

At 20 you don't know any better.

You trust them.

At 20, you have your whole life ahead of you. That's the way it's supposed to work.

•••

It was Kay who spotted the car just a few blocks from home. She didn't know what it was. Half Mustang; half something else, she guessed.

But mothers have an instinct that needs not rely on *Hot Rod Magazine* to tell them when something is special. Mothers will wake from a sound sleep and know there is a feverish brow to be cooled. Mothers will sense every danger and know the harsh truth; even though they will pretend not to see it sometimes, just so their heart will not be ripped to shreds.

Kay's instinct was dead on. She knew she had seen something special. She just wasn't quite sure what it was.

"Matty," she said, "You have got to see this car!" She called him Matty—short for Matthew—his middle name, as she had called him so many times before. Desperate times when she fought to wake him from another anesthetic sleep. Demanding the way mothers do, that he open his eyes.

"Ryan Matthew Yoder, wake up!" she would order. And Ryan always did. No matter how grim the prospects. She willed it. And he obeyed.

And now, even though it had been a very bad day, Ryan

4

knew she could not be denied. But he also knew that what she had seen was probably not special. Even at 15, when you've lived a lifetime with a disease with more syllables than an Italian menu, when you're one of just three in a million who has an affliction that leaves your intestines worthless, lucky days are few and far between.

"Mom, I don't think I can make it," he said. But Kay cajoled and comforted and finally he slumped in the passenger seat the way you would if you'd spent most of your 15 years dying.

When he spotted the car, he sat up straight. It had vent windows.

They couldn't park closer than 150 feet, but the boy whose wheelchair had been left behind demanded to get closer. So he walked 150 feet.

One hundred fifty grueling steps.

One hundred fifty agonizing steps, leaning on Kay.

One hundred fifty of the sweetest steps of his life.

Walking never came easy. Kay and Philip had to teach Ryan five or six times because the boy would be flat on his back for such interminable stretches, his body just forgot how to put one foot in front of the other.

The car was for sale, but the woman who answered the door said her son—it was his car—wouldn't be home for a couple hours. Kay made her promise not to sell the car before she and Ryan returned.

At home, if he could have, Ryan would have paced. "You have to call Dad and tell him to come home! I just know they're going to sell that car before we get back."

So Philip left his job at Eli Lilly, where they make cures for a thousand different diseases so awful they'd make your hair stand on end, where they make the pills that will cure a million boys, but not his son. Phil came home right away. "Anything to keep Ryan going another day," Kay says.

That was the day Ryan Matthew Yoder hit the jackpot. He got the car, vents and all, and when he drove his Camaro, the wind whipped past his grin.

The engine was rebuilt. Step by step, piece by chrome piece, Ryan massaged the car into something special. What Ryan was too weak to do, he directed from a lawn chair. "I put in the chrome alternator," Kay chuckles. Even the bars that steady the front fenders under the hood were replaced with chrome. When the storm clouds of winter peeked over the horizon, the car was tucked safely away and Ryan demanded that the tires be changed, so the good ones would not rot from sitting. Once, the Camaro won Best of Show—and that was before it was even finished.

•••

For eight years after the mistake, Mike Carlsen knew where his car was. He would see it go by and he would bite his lip. But 12 years ago, it slipped away forever.

Lisa Carlsen had heard the lament for years, and now with Mike's 40th birthday approaching, she set out to find a '67 Camaro. But they are hard to find—darn near impossible— because wise men do not sell '67 Camaros.

Not unless there is a very good reason.

But on the Internet one night, Lisa found one in Indiana. And when Mike left town for a weekend business trip, she left, too, for Indiana.

•••

Chronic Intestinal Pseudo Obstruction with Hirschsprungs is a death sentence. But Ryan had set all sorts of records for living, and Dr. Tim Weber set all sorts of records for keeping him alive. There were 65 major surgeries. "We quit counting the minor ones long ago," Kay wryly laughed, the sort of laugh that comes out when you feel like crying.

Funny thing about mothers. They can sense that the blur of a car they see as they drive by is the very thing that her son must have at that moment. But mothers can be blind to the writing on the wall. They will look right through looming tragedy because maybe it will go away.

6

And for a long time it worked. No matter how dire his condition, Matty always came through it. And when the call for the multi-organ transplant came from Miami, you just had to figure Ryan would make it. And if it worked... if it worked... well, life would get normal—if anyone in the Yoder household had any inkling of what normal was.

The intestines, the stomach, the pancreas, the whole transplant, went well. But there were complications and then an infection so severe, they started measuring Ryan's chances in fractions of percentage points.

But he had always pulled through before. Kay believed he would again until she had the dream—that weird, ominous dream. When she awoke, she called Philip back in Bargersville with their daughter, Renee. "You have to come back," she said.

•••

"They told us if he saw kindergarten, he would be lucky," Kay remembers. So maybe Ryan Yoder was lucky after all. Maybe that explains why he didn't complain. Never. Not once. Just took it. Took it and kept coming back.

He fought hard in the last fight. The transplant was on August 11. It was two days past Thanksgiving when he was finally counted out.

It was Kay who decided when to end it. She had birthed him and now, 20 years later, she made the call that silenced the hiss of the respirator, that stopped the torment.

"It was hard," she says softly.

Hard.

Hard luck, you might think. But that is not the way mothers think because if they did, the tears would never end. And tears have to dry up sometime. "I think we were lucky enough to have Ryan for the 20 years we had him," she says. "For me, personally, he was the best thing I ever had."

And those who knew him, counted themselves lucky, too. He gave them perspective. When they complained of a headache or a tough day on the job, they would catch themselves and remember Ryan. And if he never complained, well, how could they?

•••

It was hard selling the car. Kay wanted to keep it, but just the same, she couldn't bear to look at it.

You have to move on.

But after she handed the keys to Lisa Carlsen, she asked one favor. "I hope you don't mind if I call once in a while to see how the car is doing..."

•••

"No gifts," the invitations read. "I don't want the gag gifts and the stupid black balloons," Mike said. He's a no-nonsense kind of guy, the kind of thing you look for in a funeral director.

You wouldn't want to play poker with Mike. He's impassive. Doesn't show emotion. Won't tip his hand. He has seen terrible things. Sadnesses so grave, it could rip you up if you opened your heart to it. They do not pay undertakers to mourn. There are always enough mourners.

We gathered at the front of the lake cabin after supper, about 70 of us, and we waited, because we knew something was going to happen. Mike wondered what it was all about.

The rumble came from behind the shrubbery in the neighbor's driveway. It purred. It growled. It had vent windows.

The driver tossed the keys to Mike, and Mike stared but remained impressively impassive. That's what you would think if you did not know him. But he looked a little shaky as he slid behind the wheel of a '67 Camaro for the first time in 20 years.

He was reaching for the shifter when Lisa elbowed through the crowd, opened the passenger door and slid to the center of the seat. Mike had almost forgotten her. His arm draped around her shoulder like it had before three kids, Honda Preludes and polyester slacks, and they drove out of view as we listened to the rumble in the cooling summer dusk.

He didn't say a word, and Lisa waited for some sort of reaction, some indication of joy, some sign that this gift was truly

8

special. He pulled over a half block away and Lisa wondered, "What's wrong?"

Mike pulled up the bottom of his sweatshirt, and out of sight, where only Lisa could witness, he wiped his eyes so he could see.

After the car was parked, in hushed, reverent tones, we admired the gleaming chrome of the Camaro. Mike stared, transfixed, and maybe a little stunned.

"It really rumbles," I said.

"You know," Mike said, his eyes wide in realization, "I don't think I even heard it." He reached through the window and turned the key. The most glorious growl barked from the pipes, and the car rocked softly to the pulsating pistons.

We listened for a long time. Mike couldn't take his eyes off the car.

Not this time.

Not again.

He's going to finish what Ryan started. There are hints of rust on the trunk. The upholstery needs a little work. He will do what Ryan would have done if he had not been lashed to feeding tubes for hours and days at a time. If he had not spent most of his life in hospitals, fighting for the next moment.

Maybe Mike will change the white paint to blue like his first Camaro. But the mends and the fixes will not be done in some mad rush. It will happen slowly. He will savor these moments because he realizes what he has.

Too many things can end at 20.

Lives.

Youth.

Hope.

But sometimes, oh so very rarely, you get another chance.

© Tony Bender, 2001

The House
David Built

The wind was so fierce, it peeled the office building that housed the truck scale off the elevator in Venturia. At the Miles Miller farm, it rolled the metal roof off the cattle barn like you would open a sardine can.

Mighty trees burst from the pressure of winds pushing 100 mph. Thick trunks shattered. Branches littered the streets.

But at our house, the young trees whipped in the wind, strong and resilient. That's the way it is in life. When you are young, you are almost impervious to mighty storms and body blows. But when you are older, they can do you in.

At our house, the newly-planted 14-foot Marshall ash, the linden, the apple and the maple trees stood firm, and I was pleased.

We had them hauled in from a nursery nearly 100 miles away because the other 30 small trees The Redhead has planted in the three years we have owned the house are not for us. They will provide shade only for the next generation, I had complained.

It got me thinking. That is how David must have felt. This was his house. This is where he and Donna planned to retire.

"We were going to retire on the farm," Donna remembers. So they built across the road from the old house, away from the barn, on five pristine acres. A shelter belt was planted to the west and to the north to protect the new home.

It was done right, built stronger, with more attention to detail than you come to expect in modern homes, our carpenter has noted more than once. Roofs for miles around have come and gone, destroyed by ruinous North Dakota wind and hail. David Miller's house never lost a shingle.

They moved in just in time for the Christmas of 1976, David, Donna, Mark and Miles, and things were good. The smell of saw-dust and new paint must have still been fresh in the air.

But in 1982, David noticed a weakness in his right leg, and then in his hand, and it slowed him down something awful. By 1983 they knew the truth. Amytrophic lateral sclerosis. Lou Gehrig's disease. By 1984, David was on a respirator. A machine did what his atrophied muscles could not. It breathed for him.

It is a terrible affliction. It takes everything, every muscle, and at the end David could not talk. He could only blink as Donna pointed to the alphabet, laboriously, letter by letter, spelling out the words David wanted to say.

Donna converted the dining room into a bedroom, so he could look out to the east through the large window where pick-ups passed by, raising dust on the gravel road, or through the patio doors leading to the deck on the south side of the house, where a million sunflowers bloom today, a most perfect flower garden.

It wasn't fair, I think sometimes, that this should be the reward for a life's hard work. I see David sometimes, in my mind, and I see Donna by his side, feeding him, comforting him, for better or worse. For the worst.

Though the carpet is new, I still see in my mind the spot by his bed worn thin by Donna's footsteps.

"It is such a slow awful process," she says. Most victims of ALS live five years. But David hung on, with Donna there for every breath, until 1993. He was remarkably strong. Lou Gehrig, the Iron Horse himself, lasted just two years after he pulled him-

11

self out of the Yankee lineup eight games into the 1939 season.

In the last months, David could no longer blink, and he could only look into Donna's eyes, and she into his. It is cruel, this disease. It takes everything, but it spares your vision and your mind, so you will know what you have lost.

After the struggle was over and that wretched disease had finally won, Miles recalls walking into the house that David built.

The steady hiss of the respirator had gone silent. "It was eerie." And it was lonely. Out here, when winter sets in, grey and bitter, you can feel so very alone.

Sadness had permeated the walls. It lived there in the house.

It was Miles who called when he saw the ad in the paper. We were moving to McIntosh County and we needed a home.

The Redhead loved the big windows, the light warming the expansive rooms. She loved the elbow room in the yard.

But I felt the sorrow in the house as Donna offered the tour. It was melancholy, this place.

"I had to start a new life," Donna told me. "I couldn't do it out there any more. It was the past."

In 1998, a little more than a month after seeing the house, we moved in. Slowly we made it our own. The sadness retreated, driven away by the exuberant chatter of our boy Dylan, and then, last year, by the coos and smiles of our little girl, India.

The house began to breathe again and every day, when I drive into the yard, I am pleased by our progress.

"It's a happy place again," I told Donna just an hour after Dylan's fifth birthday party, after the last handful of children had headed home.

"I'm sure the children run from the dining room to the kitchen to the living room just like our grandchildren did," Donna said, a catch in her throat.

"Yes," I said. And I told her how I think of David, how I see him in my mind some days and how sometimes I mourn the unfairness of it all.

12

"We will have to have you over," I told her. And I told her of the things we had changed, and I told her about the trees.

"We have done..."

"You have done," she interrupted, "what we would have done."

© Tony Bender, 2001

Soul of
Venturia

When Mata Hari—the band, not the spy—got out of the bus
and looked around, they wondered where they were.

"We're here," said Bobby Delzer. "This is it."

Indeed.

By the second night of the two-night stand, after death
threats had reached their booking agent, the band had packed
in people the way Norwegians pack in kippered snacks, and they
smiled down from the Doghouse stage.

"You couldn't move," Bobby remembers, a naughty glint in
his eye, "You couldn't really dance. You just had to sort of hop
up and down."

T. J. Haerich had just moved to town, and he remembers
coming down Venturia's crumbling main drag to find 300 revel-
ers spilled out into the street. "I wondered what I'd gotten myself
into."

But the Doghouse—it used to be City Hall—hasn't hosted a
concert in years. The Venturia City Council saw to that.

Oh, you can still hear a country song or two on the jukebox
at the Duck Inn, the last business in town—if you don't count
the Baptist church.

If you like it quiet, the Duck Inn is perfect. There's just the
creak of the floor as you shift in your stool, the ringing of the

glass as Eddie Ackerman plunks ice into a Lord Calvert and Coke.

Drinking with the Lord, they call it around here, on the opposite and far end of the street from the church.

Fifty years ago, the community boasted a score of businesses. Now the Venturia Centennial Committee, larger in number than the actual population of 25, gathers in last-minute, worried huddles before Saturday's Centennial.

It should be quite a blast.

This is how they face the end. With a party. So many other towns have long ago melted. Dried up and blown away. But here they cling doggedly with fingernails. It's not that they don't see the end. It's the way things are in North Dakota today, but scarce is the politician who dares admit it. In Venturia, denial isn't an option. It is what it is. The motto of the Centennial, emblazoned boldly on the 112 page centennial book? "Almost gone but not forgotten."

At the intersections of Highways 11 and 3, most cars turn north to Wishek or continue on to Ashley or Hague depending on which way the front bumper is pointed.

But a few do go south, the ones headed to Eureka, or the ones headed to see Eddie or to church.

There's a a rock pile to the east, halfway down the two mile stretch of two-lane blacktop. A boulder squats in the middle of the other rocks, painted in black and white, the words mourning the lost in Vietnam. There's a flag pole, but usually no flag. Alberta Clippers see to that.

If you go straight, you'll hit gravel, then dirt, and then you will find the cemetery where buffalo grass anchors the soil, a dusty, faded green carpet over the graves.

If you turn west, and most people do, you will see the garish, hand painted sign in yellow and red. Fresh Eggs!

Half a block up and to the north is the lumber yard. Faded. Leaning a bit, but still standing, leaded glass windows and all.

Take a left, but be careful. They park in the middle of the

15

street outside the Duck Inn. City Hall still stands to the east, but Wes Schlepp owns it now, and the rock and roll does not play in Venturia any more.

The post office is closed, white paint peeling. T.J. says it ought to be painted before the Centennial, but he's got his hands full repainting the old Soo Line depot.

It's quiet, but on Sundays the traffic increases as two dozen, or three on a good day, slide into the pews. Pastor Tschetter is asked how the congregation is doing on the new song—the tricky one. "You know, the one we can't sing."

"We have a lot of those," he chuckles. But truth be told, most days the singing rings clear and joyous. It's a fact. The Venturia Baptists can outsing the Lutherans who are in the majority out here.

That's just the way it is.

© Tony Bender, 2001

Editor's note: Venturia celebrated its centennial on June 30, 2001.

Tractor Freak Show

After the muffler fell off my 1952 Ford tractor and was chopped to shreds by the attached Farm King mower, I knew the repair was beyond my ability.

Besides, I figured, while I had it in the shop, they could tighten the brakes and replace the non-standard generator that required a broomstick to provide the proper tension for the fan belt.

The broomstick was Randy Ulmer's idea. I called him when the tractor started overheating, and since he sold it to me, he felt obligated to check it out.

He peered in at the makeshift generator set-up.

"That ain't right!" he said.

At this point, I discovered that Randy's mechanical expertise rivals mine. It scared the heck out of me.

When the first tool a guy reaches for is a hammer, it's not a good sign. But he pounded the broomstick into place and it worked like a charm. "It's been Ulmerized!" he declared in the manner of a priest granting absolution.

Despite his success, I was reluctant to have him help fix the muffler, lest the repair involve lumber. But he did haul the tractor to the Cenex station for me.

At this point, for those who missed the first installment of the *Tractor Chronicles*, I must explain that the tractor caused a minor sensation out here in farm country when Randy trucked it in, because, well, no one around here had ever seen anything quite like it.

The dignified original gray and red Ford colors had been abandoned, and it had been bathed in Caterpillar yellow, now chipped and sullied by the years. Attached to the front of this little 8-N Ford is an oversized 6-foot bucket. At best, it's homely.

So you can understand why a crowd gathered as it was unloaded. Word gets around. *"Free tractor freak show at the gas station!"*

Head mechanic Bobby Delzer listened to my instructions but was unable to make eye contact. He just grunted as he stared at his next project.

He studied the generator.

"That ain't right," he asserted.

It was there for about two weeks. Bobby said he was having trouble getting his hands on the proper generator.

But when I stopped in for a Coke, I saw a man approach Bobby, huddling secretively. He slipped Bobby a buck, and they disappeared into the shop. Moments later, shrieks of laughter reverberated through the lobby. Other customers smirked, winked and shared knowing nods.

When I went to settle up for the repairs a few days later, Bobby told me he had taken the tractor to Ehley's Blacksmith Shop to study the generator set up.

"What'd he say?" I asked.

18

"He said it ain't right," Bobby answered. "Wanna know how I finally got it to work?"

I did.

"Stuck a block of wood behind it."

I wondered how much I owed him.

"Nadda. We wouldn't feel good about taking your money. We made enough charging admission to fund the Christmas party," he confessed.

I gassed it up and drove it the 12 miles home. Even in road gear, it plodded along. Along the way—*I swear this is the absolute truth*—a bumble bee flew up, attempting, I think, to mate with my bee-colored tractor. When its amorous advances were ignored, the bee huffed a bit, then flew off passing the tractor.

The tractor worked fine until I hit that badger hole again, dislodging Bobby's block of wood.

The next day, I marched into McCleary Lumber.

"Watcha need?"

"A part for my tractor."

"Implement dealer's right across the street."

"Look, don't argue. Just cut me a wedge of wood about eight inches long."

It cost me 50 cents and it works fine.

© Tony Bender, 2000

Weed Nazis

I'm not saying I wasn't in the wrong. But the penalty was a lot like using a sledge hammer to swat flies.

When Grandpa Ben left that 75 acres of idled crop land to us Bender kids, I never imagined it would lead to a run-in with the Weed Nazis.

As the proud owner of 12.5 of those acres, I suppose I should have studied the contract a little more carefully before signing, along with my siblings, another CRP (Could Really be a Problem) contract.

Signing a treaty with the U.S. Government never worked out all that well for the Lakota, so I don't know what led me to believe I could do better. But I didn't see anything in there about killing all my buffalo and wiping out my tribe with smallpox, so I fell for it.

Signing up for CRP is a lot like selling your soul to the devil, except with the devil, the worst that can happen is burning in agony amongst the brimstone and sulphur in eternal damnation. Compared to the Weed Nazis, Satan is a piker.

Minutes after signing, I got a letter from the Weed Gestapo advising me to cut or spray the weeds on the CRP.

Or else.

This sort of surprised me because after driving around and

studying other CRP land, I had come to the conclusion that CRP was sort of a refuge for weeds—kinda like a national grassland.

Some day our Canadian thistle will go the way of the wooly mammoth and about that time someone will figure out that thistles are the key to curing warts or halitosis.

Anyway, when I did the math, I came to the startling conclusion that if we were to spray the land, we would actually lose hundreds of dollars on the acreage. When I asked around to see if that could be so, that our benevolent government would sponsor a farm program that could actually force a fellow to lose money, guys in feed store hats just smiled a wry sort of smile and gave me a secret handshake. Losing that kind of money per acre had made me an official farmer.

Fortunately, a friend clipped the offending weeds last year, but because the rough ground had bounced important parts off his equipment and because he required months of chiropractic rehabilitation afterward, he was reluctant to do the job again this year. I asked around but couldn't find a taker for the task. So I handled it like I do many of my vexing problems. I ignored it and hoped it would go away.

I'm still a little irked that it was me that had to appear before the Weed Board. But that's what happens when you're the one who lives close to the problem and your brothers and sisters all resist extradition.

Naturally, the meeting was set for a Tuesday, press day for the newspaper. Another subtle torture.

"You're not going to write about this, are you?" they asked when I walked in.

"I guess we'll have to see how it goes," I responded. The fine was $1,036. Plus it cost another $600 to get it clipped.

I'm writing about it.

Now, I'm not saying I wasn't in the wrong here, but wow, to get a traffic ticket that large, I would have to be driving drunk in the wrong lane, littering, without proof of insurance, at 518 mph.

21

"Why are you always picking on us farmers?" I whimpered. Then it was explained that under Provision 64, Section 321, of the Freedom to Farm Act, picking on farmers is mandatory.

The last time I incurred a penalty so severe was when I performed an "illegal operation" on Windows 95, and Bill Gates kicked down the door with a couple of bruisers in dark suits and sunglasses and broke my thumbs.

But I'm not bitter.

I'm not bitter about the fact that just south of the airport on federal wildlife land, there is an impressive stand of wormwood, putting the government in violation of its own noxious weed rules.

And I'm not bitter about the fact that I was ratted out by someone without the common courtesy to make a man-to-man or weasel-to-man phone call to discuss the problem. The world needs more stool pigeons, rats, finger pointers, squealers, whistle blowers and tattletales.

No, I'm not bitter. I know weeds are a bad thing and that I was wrong. And I won't let it happen again.

But I'm writing about it. After all, it's almost a free country.

And I'm not bitter.

Hell, no.

© Tony Bender, 2000

A Three Fruit
Basket Winter

When I was a teenager, my friends Whitey, Hawkeye, Gare Bear and I would play bone-jarring, teeth-rattling tackle football in the snow between my house and the Leesburg's trailer house.

If you smacked into the side of the porch on a post pattern, you were out of bounds. Of course, we didn't pass much—it was difficult with two pair of gloves on.

Usually it was bitter cold, but that had its advantages, too. When a tooth was knocked loose by one of Whitey's patented flying knee-to-your-jaw tackles, you were so numb it hardly hurt when you spat out the remains of your bicuspid.

But that was then. Nowadays, winter just ticks me off. Mostly it's the peer pressure. When it snows around here, 103-year-old invalids can be spotted with a grain scoop, clearing out three-foot drifts in -35 degree weather, from a driveway long enough to safely land a 747.

I, however, do not believe in shoveling the driveway to our rural home for the same reason I do not believe in fixing the bed in the morning—it's just going to get messed up again anyway. That is why I purchased 4x4s.

If the drifts get too deep for my Explorer, I invest in a fruit basket to be delivered to my neighbor to remind him of my great affection for him, his lovely wife, extended family, and of course, his large tractor with the snowblower attached.

The deep snow has been particularly hard on our English springer spaniel, Karma. As she wades through the snow to greet visitors, it looks like a beaver pelt being pushed along by the wind. I intend to solve this problem by getting a taller dog.

While it has only been a three fruit basket winter so far, the snow has a peculiar way of swirling around our house and placing a drift right in front of the garage doors.

I solved this problem by driving over the snowbank, compressing it over time into a solid block of ice which grew to such an embarrassing epic height, the neighborhood kids took to sledding on it.

We compassionately opened the garage doors after we saw several tykes come down Ice Mountain and flatten themselves against the doors like Wile E. Coyote into a painted tunnel on a rock wall. This mountain grew so tall it became a common sight to see Sherpa tribesmen puffing Pall Malls at base camp near the front door.

Eventually, even I had to admit something needed to be done. So I called Bill Heim, our contractor, and told him now would be a good time to put on those fancy new garage doors we'd been waiting for, knowing full-well he would have to chip away the ice mountain in order to complete the job.

Sure, the project cost more than a grand, but I have new garage doors and can still drive into the stall though I have shoveled nary a scoop this winter.

One day, the luggage rack scraped a bit, but we had a nice two-day thaw that took six inches off the bump. Near as I can figure, I'm three good snowstorms away from having to put on even newer garage doors. But with a few days of thaw and a fruit basket or two, I might make spring.

© Tony Bender, 2001

Can You Do
Any Better?

The Redhead's relatives descended upon our house last week-end—nine of them—and you know how relatives are. They must be fed.

The Redhead called Adolph at Super Valu to order 20 pounds of ribs for Sunday dinner. I stopped in Thursday to make sure the ribs had been set aside.

"Do you want them today?" he asked.

"Naw, I'll get them Saturday," I said. "Why?"

"Well, if you got them today, the price would be a little better," Adolph teased.

I didn't catch on. "Well, how much can I save?" I wondered.

Adolph, in his white butcher's apron, grinned a toothy grin and accused me of being a cheap German.

"I've been living in Ashley too long," I admitted. "I almost bought an accordion the other day, too."

Then Adolph told me a story about a real Ashley German. True story, he said.

The man walked into the lumber yard and pointed to a board. "How much do you want for that?" he demanded of the proprietor.

The lumberman surveyed the board. It was scrap. "That you can have," he told the man.

The customer scratched his chin thoughtfully. "Can you do a little better?"

But you don't have to actually be a German to acquire the demeanor. You just have to live near them all your life. Take The Redhead's family. They're Danish—originally from Daneland, for you students of geography—and meaner than a mud wasp in a dry gourd when it comes to dickering.

They're legend around here. When The Redhead was a teen, she and her dad went out to buy a Jeep. The salesman wouldn't budge, and the argument got so fierce the cops were called, and that's why The Redhead still has a record.

"Who knew thumbscrews were illegal?" her Dad complains to this day.

I was with him last fall when he walked into a dealership. "I'm Gary Lovgren, and I want to know how much you want for that Dodge!" he announced.

A cowering manager peeked up from behind the desk.

"That you can have," he said.

"He'll take it," I said before Gary could argue.

They threw in the mud flaps.

© Tony Bender, 2001

The Robbery of
Gilbert's Grave

It's amazing what you can get away with if you look like you
know what you're doing. You can march right into a North
Dakota cemetery and nab a one ton tombstone in broad daylight
in front of a dozen living witnesses and a thousand dead, and if
you don't act guilty, no one will challenge you.

This is not just a theory, mind you. It's been done. If you
travel the dusty, west river backroads to Jimmy Howe's old
ranch 19 miles southwest of Hettinger, you will see the evidence
on the east side of the gracious home, warming in the morning
sun. Many guests and the occasional rattler have seen the tombstone. Few know the story.

It wasn't really grave robbing; at least if it was, you have to
figure the statute of limitations has expired by now. Anyway,
that is what the bandit Harriet Tobin Howe has wagered.

Besides, the Gilberts are all ghosts now. There is no one left to push the issue.

The plan was hatched generations back, and when you study the family history, you can see just how irksome the behemoth stone would become, placed "katty-wampus" in the Tobin family plot where all the other stones were flat markers surrounding a proud monolith bearing the Tobin name.

First and foremost, they are Irish, these Tobins. And after Patrick T. Tobin arrived in Dakota Territory in 1881, he passed on his love of country and sense of duty to his family. "Every one of them served," Harriet says. "My family understands the meaning of democracy and what Thomas Jefferson was all about."

"I think with military people, ceremony and ritual is important—and with the Irish, too," she adds. So it was the military demand for order and thick-headed Irish pride that set the wheels in motion back in 1918 when poor Gilbert died.

Not that Everett Gilbert was a slacker, mind you. He, too, served in WWI. But the flu epidemic which marauded across continents, more formidable than the Kaiser's armies, did in the poor lad during boot camp.

Well, Patrick T. Tobin was not a dispassionate man. Knowing his sister's poverty, he offered a Tobin plot so his nephew might be properly laid to rest, and that was well and good until another benefactor placed the massive stone at the head of Gilbert's grave without permission.

Like a wart the size of a walnut on a pretty girl's forehead, it tortured the Tobins. One day, when all the Gilberts were gone—and the Tobins were determined to outlast them all—the stone must be removed.

At family gatherings, the children heard the mutterings and the complaints and the vow. As generations faded, the task of removing the blight from the family plot in the Mandan cemetery fell to their successors.

When Patrick T. passed on, and then Harriet's grandfather, the task fell to her father. "And then my dad dies," Harriet says.

28

"It was almost like whoever was left is where the blame could be placed."

So the Tobins waited for the Gilberts to die. But your average Gilbert is not so easily dispatched. Aunt Pearl was a hardy gal, and had bad luck visited the dwindling Tobins once or twice, she might have outlasted them. But finally, a dozen years past, at the age of 97, stubborn Pearl died.

Harriet's second cousin, Marguerite Tobin Chase, and her husband, Les, flew out from Long Island, NY, to be there the day a Montana grave digger, who asked no questions, winched the stone into Jimmy Howe's sturdy truck.

Uncle Dave and Auntie Colleen Tobin Connelly of Bismarck were there, too.

"We all converged at the Mandan Union Cemetery in broad daylight," Harriet says, more than a little gleeful as she recounts the caper. "It was a beautiful summer day. People were bringing flowers to graves. Caretakers were watering bushes, and no one stopped to wonder."

Like Aunt Pearl, Gilbert did not give up easy. The base of the monument was buried deep and Auntie Colleen remembers, "We had a helluva time getting the stone out."

But finally they did, and Harriet and Jimmy Howe drove laboriously and unchallenged back to Hettinger with the truck's nose pointed skyward under Gilbert's weight.

A modest flat marker replaced the monstrosity which now hunkers among the buttes and coulees and pale green buffalo grass, a mystery to those who visit the ranch.

Not that folks didn't ask, because even in a land where independent thinkers and doers are the norm, hardly anyone has a tombstone for a lawn ornament out by the pink plastic flamingoes.

But to explain it all, that would get tedious, Jimmy decided.

So when the inevitable query would come, he would tilt back the brim of his hat and stare mournfully out across the grassland, and in his booming west river twang he would simply explain, "Gilbert was my favorite horse."

Cowboys have always loved great horses, haven't they? Trigger was stuffed for cripes sakes. You could not doubt his sincerity. Such was Jimmy's carriage that no one ever dared probe further into his reverie.

Alas, poor Gilbert.

© Tony Bender, 2001

Benches

Anyone who grew up in a small town has seen the changes. Stores close one by one. The young move away in search of jobs while the elderly seem to fade away.

The one thing I miss the most is the benches that lined Main Street. They were placed there by the merchants as a resting place for the old men, an unspoken invitation that was accepted daily. You'd see them there in bib overalls, the uniform of the day. In the morning, they'd bask in the sun and later, when it got too hot, they would migrate to the shade on the other side of the street.

The benches hosted countless debates and world's problems were solved daily.

Dogs stretched out on the cool sidewalk in front of their masters. Kids wandered by and offered distractions. Some stopped, but most continued on their way.

I was one of those who stopped to listen.

Sometimes there was nothing to hear but the creaking bones of old men who were all talked out or just content with the silence and their memories.

Werner Groop would roll a smoke with Tip-Top papers and Prince Albert in a can, when the conversation lagged. Dale Doty might excuse himself for a 10 a.m. beer, served in a graceful Hamms glass by Bob Hahn in the Ponderosa Bar. Dale was tall, maybe 6-4, and as a crown to his blue and white striped Key coveralls, he wore an engineer's hat, the brim flipped back so that it seemed to wink and broadcast his good humor, worthless in the sun. Dale always tossed a sprinkle of salt in the beer, and it would sink almost to the bottom, even as the bubbles it raised floated to the top. The glass was small in his grip of iron, even into his eighties, a grip exercised each week as he raised 55 gallon drums of garbage high into the bed of the forties-something Plymouth truck he used to haul the townsfolk's trash.

I stopped because these were my friends. Most of the kids my age were putting in long days on the farm. So by default I became an honorary old man.

Life takes on a different tilt when your buddies are 60 or 70 years older than you. They didn't want to discuss girls or sports unless it was Heddy Lemar or Stan Musial, so for the most part, I listened to the halting rhythms, the stories told with twinkling eyes under wrinkled brows. I listened and learned obscure histories.

My parents and friends never really knew about my secret life as an old man. It was a part of my life I took for granted on those lazy summer days, in a special little town, never realizing in the moment, the gift. Now I know so well what I had, what a perfect place in time it was.

These old men were like treasure chests filled with rich memories if only you could find the key. Some locks were rusty, but with patience, the golden memories would emerge shining.

I'm not sure when those old wooden benches disappeared. The paint faded and the wood cracked. It happened so slowly that no one noticed.

And then they were gone like so many of their occupants.

I miss those old guys and I miss those benches.

•••

Today, I have four benches at home to honor friends long gone but not forgotten. At my office, in front in the shade, is another bench. Once in a while, I will spy someone, maybe a child, maybe an old man in overalls, sitting on that bench.

I always smile because things are as they should be.

© Tony Bender, 1991, revised in 2001.

What Do You Believe?

"What do you believe?" he asked me at the church picnic, after the baked beans, hot dishes and chocolate cakes were satisfyingly lodged in my gullet, after belts had surreptitiously been loosed another notch.

I thought about it for a moment as the children romped in the park, as the grip of autumn began to win her battle with summer.

"I believe in reincarnation," I said. "I believe we are all connected, that the train to realization cannot arrive at the final destination until everyone is on board. I believe in Buddha. And Krishna. And Moses. And Jesus. And maybe the Dalai Lama but not in Richard Gere. And I believe I'll have a beer.

"I believe what goes around, comes around. As you sow, so shall ye reap. I believe in Karma. I believe an eye for an eye. I believe in turning the other cheek. I believe in a loving God, not a smiting God. I believe in Grace. Not the baseball player, although he's good.

"I believe Moses parted the Red Sea. That Jesus turned water into wine and that he raised Lazarus. I believe DiMaggio hit in 57 straight. I believe the designated hitter is a mistake and that Pete Rose should not be in the Hall of Fame and that instead of using Ty Cobb as a bellwether, he should be tossed out, too.

"I believe thoughts are things," I said as the children tossed water balloons, giggling, running with the conditioning of marathoners. "I believe thoughts have the power to help or harm," I said. "I believe prayer works.

"I believe there is no death, but I fear a painful one. I believe in life. I believe I have known you in another life but that it is this life, not that one, when you were Napoleon and I was a court jester, that is important.

"I believe Shirley Maclaine is right about more things than you might guess. I believe the earth is sliding on its axis, that the poles are shifting and that you can see it in the change in the weather. But I don't believe it means the end of the world.

"I believe, even living in farm country, that I would do better not to eat meat. I believe I'll take my steak rare.

"I believe you can dissolve clouds with your mind, if you think you can. I believe in '67 Chevies and 327 short blocks and four-barrel carbs and manual transmissions. I believe in the Vikings but not in the Red Sox.

"I believe we are all on a journey, all aiming for the same destination, but that the paths are as varied as the stars in the nighttime sky.

"I do not believe people in the rain forest must be baptized to be saved but that it gives you clean hair. I believe in hymns set to the tune of old drinking songs. I believe Martin Luther liked a good snort.

"I believe I am a hypocrite. Ill tempered. Small thinking and entirely salvageable by God.

"I think we make too much of church and forget to see the divine as we walk across sweet, green bluegrass to water the saplings.

"I do not believe in hell or the devil, but I sometimes feel a negative energy around me so powerful it frightens me. I believe in the Loch Ness Monster and in giant squids and in Gandhian non-violent protest. I believe in orderly anarchy.

"I believe what I believe in isn't important. It is what you

35

believe that is. I do not believe I will be judged by others but that I will judge myself and that I fear the verdict.

"I believe I could attain enlightenment in a moment but that it will probably take more lifetimes. I believe the Lakota, the Blackfoot, Shoshone, Chickasaw and Cherokee know God.

"I believe Jimmy Swaggart is insane and Falwell is a fraud but Billy Graham is not. I believe my dog is not really lost or dead but sitting in front of a warm hearth with a kindly family, stealing table scraps and smiling the way dogs do. And I believe Duck Dog misses me but does not know how to get home and, anyway, is getting too old to do it.

"I believe my mother is imperfect, and it pains me because I did not believe it for years and now she is one of us. I believe Mother Teresa is a saint but Princess Di was not. I believe Prince Charles has very big ears and should marry again if it makes him happy. I believe the English need better dental care.

"I believe *Goodbye Yellow Brick Road* was Elton's best but *Tumbleweed Connection* is in the running. I believe in George Carlin and Robin Williams and Chris Rock and Dennis Miller and Eddie Izzard but not in Drew Carey.

"I believe the French should lighten up on Americans. After all, we saved their bacon in WWII. But they saved ours in 1776, so I suppose we're even.

"I believe in the prairie. In elbow room. In looking them in the eye. I believe in left hooks to the jaw and knees to the groin. And I believe in handshakes and hugs.

"I believe in Jung, not Freud and not Nietzsche. I believe in Zen. In Mohammed and Saint Peter and Saint Nick.

"I believe in the Easter Bunny but not Peter Cottontail hopping down the bunny trail.

"I believe you are right and that I am, too. I believe I'd rather fight than switch, but I won't walk a mile for a Camel.

"I believe in the wisdom of children and fear the folly of wrinkled old men. I believe in puppies and kittens but not in hamsters or gerbils.

36

"I believe in my wife and she believes in me and we both believe in Tom T. Hall and little baby ducks.

"I believe in driving fast in a Mustang ragtop on a deserted road on a summer day, but the McIntosh County Sheriff's Department does not.

"I believe in hard red spring wheat and canola and flax. I believe our farmers are not getting a fair shake and it will cost us all.

"I believe the real danger is not big government but big business or both when they have no conscience. I believe our stock market investments further more wrongs than rights, and I wish my tech fund would bounce back.

"I believe in getting things done. I believe in taking time off. I believe in sunshine and rain but not in Democrats or Republicans.

"I believe there was an Atlantis and that our technology pales in comparison, and I suppose there must be life out there somewhere.

"I believe in Ella and Sarah and the Count but not the Duke. I believe in Mel Torme and Sinatra and Tony Bennett but not in Perry Como, Andy Williams or the Ray Conniff Singers.

"I believe all you need is love and the air that I breathe, that he ain't heavy, he's my brother and that the answer is blowing in the wind.

"I believe in reaching far and that it is forgivable to fall short. I believe in going with the flow and tilting against windmills. I believe in serenity. I believe in war sometimes but almost never.

"What do you believe?" I asked, looking up.

But he was not there.

© Tony Bender, 2001

I was about two when my Grandpa and Grandma Spilloway came for a visit. Grandma had chickens back then and she brought a donation—a pail of farm fresh eggs for my mom.

Grandpa absently set the pail in my wagon which was parked in the front porch where all my toys were kept. I was playing in the yard.

A while later, Grandpa peeked into the porch and there I was, carefully removing the eggs, one by one, cracking them on the pail and emptying the contents into the wagon.

I don't know how long he watched, shaking with mirth, but knowing Grandpa, it was probably a good while. Shells littered the floor as I pushed the slimy goo around the wagon with my tiny fingers.

"Come here," Grandpa whispered to Grandma and Mom.

"Oh for Pete's sake!" my very practical grandma exclaimed, moving to stop the destruction.

"Let him go!" Grandpa ordered softly.

"She can bring you more eggs," he told my mom.

Tony Bender
Scrambled eggs, 1995

The Redhead and Me

She started testing me with all sorts of what-if scenarios. Like what would I do if Kim Bassinger burst into my living room, stripped off her Frederick's of Hollywood nightie and said, "Take me, stud." That's plausible. Let's see, that has happened to me exactly...NEVER.

"I would be true, my dear," I told The Redhead. "I would call the police and shout, 'Begone, harlot!'

That's what I told her anyway.

Tony Bender
Can't Figure Out Women, 1993

Messy Guy

It never fails. Whenever I go out in public, I end up a mess.

It's not that I haven't tried. I have. I avoid having the ribs at a cafe. Or I wear an orange shirt. But I always end up walking around with so much food on my clothes, it is not unusual for me to be stalked by entire herds of dogs and cats.

When I go camping, after supper my friends dangle me on a rope between two trees so the bears won't get me.

Recently, when The Redhead and I went to a swank Denver restaurant with friends, I ordered the mussels and linguini with white wine sauce. So .06 nanoseconds into the meal, I had wine sauce on the front of my green silk shirt. It was pretty bad.

After dinner, when I had finished rubbing the cheesecake around on my chest, my friend Bob asked, "Where should we go next?"

"Someplace dark," The Redhead said.

On the way to the Comedy Works, we were stopped by a panhandler.

"Can I have some money for a sandwich?" he asked.

"I'm sorry. I don't have any change." I said.

"Can I at least lick your shirt?" he wondered.

At this point I would like to offer some useful advice. Sitting in front at a comedy club with a stained shirt is not a good idea. Most of the time, when I pay $20 for public humiliation, I at least get to eat.

As we drove home from Denver that weekend, The Redhead ordered me to kill a pesky fly. She hates flies.

I should have let the fly live.

After he landed on me, I gave him a swat and splashed coffee on my khaki shirt.

So when we pulled into a Nebraska truck stop, I headed to the rest room to clean up. I had just finished redistributing the coffee stain on my shirt, when I noticed the dark brown stain on the front of my shorts. Even I can't go out in public like that. I didn't want to get my underwear wet as I scrubbed the stain on my groin, so I put one hand in my pants as I scrubbed with the other.

That is what I was doing at the sink by the door when the large, bearded trucker walked in. He took one look and slowly backed out of the room.

If they had only mounted the hand drier lower, I could have used it to dry the massive wet spot on my groin.

I tried to maintain my dignity as I walked out. I looked everyone in the eye except for the trucker, who was apparently calling the authorities at the pay phone. When I got to the car which was at the gas pumps, it was locked. And The Redhead was gone. So I stood there with this big wet spot on my crotch as folks pumped gas around me. I know what they were thinking.

One guy just kept staring.

Like there was something wrong with me.

I was very irritated.

By the time The Redhead returned, I had had enough.

"OK," I loudly announced to the gaping gas pumpers. "I wet my pants! Are you happy now? Is that what you wanted to hear?"

I was very glad to leave Nebraska.

© Tony Bender, 2001

Mexican
Tribulations

There are no rules in Mexican driving. This one of many interesting facts The Redhead and I learned during our trip south
of the border. In fact, there are hardly any Mexicans in Mexico.
They have moved to Los Angeles, and the French have taken
over.

Despite the trepidation in our travel agent's voice, we boldly
insisted on renting a car to get around.

So moments after clearing immigration in Cancun, we were
careening wildly in a green van to the rental car place where
they outfitted us with a Volkswagen Beetle.

We soon learned that all tourists must drive Beetles. It's the
law. It makes identification of tourists much easier. Another
good way to to identify tourists is by the number of fresh dents
in the vehicle.

After being pointed in the general direction of town, we set
out to find our hotel, the name of which had been cryptically
described by our travel agent as "starting with a C."

The first 45 minutes of being lost wasn't too bad. I had
learned to cut off other drivers just like the taxies. We had also
learned a lot of Mexican sign language.

"Why are all those cars honking at us?" asked The Redhead.

"Just being friendly," I said. "They love tourists."

In our third hour in the non-air conditioned Beetle, The Redhead's curls were getting limp, and she explained that the novelty of being lost was wearing thin. We had driven by 117 hotels all starting with a "C." After all this was Cancun.

Everyone knows that men are genetically predisposed to *not ask* for directions. That is why many experts believe Jimmy Hoffa isn't really dead. He just refuses to pull over and ask for directions back to Jersey.

But in the interest of male evolution and the resurrection of The Redhead's waning affection, I decided to ask for directions.

The first couple I stopped looked at me disdainfully and replied in French. I responded by reciting the lyrics to *Michelle (My Belle)*.

They responded by looking at me as if I was some sort of idiot.

Of all the luck. If I had wanted to get insulted by snooty French people, I would have gone to France.

The next couple I asked replied in German. Thus I learned fact number two about Mexico. Absolutely none of the Caucasians in Mexico are Americans.

So I pulled into the next hotel I could find where the Mexican doorman explained in perfect English that I was really lost. Fortunately, a taxi driver was parked nearby. I got him to lead us to our hotel. It cost me five bucks and my little remaining pride.

The sight of two sweaty tourists in a rental car being led by a taxi to the door of the hotel was a source of great amusement for the doorman. But in the interest of a tip, he managed to suppress his giggles. However, in the crowded elevator, he regaled other passengers with the tale of our undistinguished arrival. At least I think that is what he was doing. They all just nodded and grinned at us. I responded by reciting the lyrics to *Michelle (My Belle)*, so they would think I was French.

The service was great. They thought I was Paul McCartney.

The trip to the ancient city of Chichen Itza was fairly

44

uneventful. However, there were heavily-armed soldiers posted along the way. I am fairly certain it is their job to kill snooty French people, and I am with them on that all the way.

In Chichen, we learned many things about this Pre-Columbian society, including the fact that these Mayans were there long before Columbus discovered Pancho Villa.

Our guide, Javiar, insisted we climb the massive pyramid at the beginning of the tour. Only about 17 percent of tourists actually survive the trip up and down. Javiar waited at the bottom with the other tour guides. When a body would tumble down, they would carefully remove the appropriate amount of pesos from the mangled corpse to cover the cost of the abbreviated tour. "No refunds, Senor."

Our hotel at Chichen had all the amenities including a pet scorpion, which I drop-kicked off the porch through two palm trees. The real Twilight Zone episode involved a King Spider. When I smashed the silver-dollar sized arachnid, it seemed to explode into hundreds of tiny spiders. We found out later that mother King Spiders carry their young on the underside of their bodies. It took a five-minute tap dance to get them all.

"Are they poisonous?" I asked Javiar the next day.

"Not very," he replied.

The experts aren't really sure what happened to the Mayans. It might have been the King Spiders. Or the French.

At the motel, I was stopped by yet another French tourist.

"Do... you... know... where... the... pool... is?" he asked in perfect English, speaking as if I was a moron.

"Bonus Notches," I said. "Cinco de Mayo cervaza El Segundo Zorro."

Puzzled, he threw up his arms and walked away.

Stupid French.

© Tony Bender, 1996

Perfect Day

She was late. Dylan had been two weeks and 10 pounds 4 ounces late. The Redhead certainly didn't want to go through *that* again.

"Is tomorrow a good day to have a baby?" she asked from her cell phone on her way back from her doctor's office. Of course it was! Are you kidding? I was beyond anxious to see our little girl. Earlier that week, I tapped on The Redhead's tummy and leaned over. "Hello? Are you coming out soon?" Though I listened carefully, there was no reply.

After the call, I wasn't worth a hoot at the office, but distracted, I cheerfully bumbled through the afternoon.

We traveled the 90 miles to Aberdeen that night in anticipation of the 5:30 a.m. appointment. The plan was to induce labor. But from the motel shower, my sweetie informed me that she had been having contractions since midnight and we had best move along.

We were blocked by a 100 car train on our way to the hospital. Perfect. At the admissions desk we discovered the paperwork wasn't there. So much for preregistration.

As the two women dawdled behind the desk in the deserted waiting room, I grew impatient. "Would it make a difference if I told you my wife is in labor?" I asked. The lady smiled politely and shooed me away. One must have a sucking chest wound to avoid the initial paperwork.

I had just finished telling the same old lie to my wife at 11:13 a.m.—*just one more push*—and our family had grown to four.

Our baby howled, indignant, at the poking and prodding. At 11:15 I kissed my bride and nonchalantly asked, "Wanna do this again?"

She howled louder than the baby.

I wanted Dylan, at Grandma Jan and Grandpa Jim's, to hear the news, and I wondered how he would take it.

His mother, the center of his life, had worried, too. But she resolved she would not succumb—anymore than usual, anyway—to sympathy for the lad. A few days earlier our bouncing-off-the-walls boy was an inch from another time out, his exasperated mother warned.

"Let him go," I chided. "After all, he's only going to be king for a couple more days."

The baby's cries, and my smiles, continued as I dialed the number. At my mother's first "hello" I choked up, unable to express my joy, so all she heard was an angry nine pound debutante giving the staff what-for.

"Do you hear something?" I finally managed.

"Oh, Ohh, Ohhhh!" she stuttered, choking up herself. For a moment, the only sounds to travel the phone line were those of protest from my little girl.

"She's very loud..." I said before choking up again... "And she's perfect."

I composed myself as Dylan came to the phone. "Dylan, you are a big brother. You have a new sister!" The phone thudded and there was a faint "yippie" as the boy twirled in joy.

The next day, when we picked up Dylan, we buckled him into his car seat in the back, where he has ridden a thousand miles looking at the back of our heads. When I buckled his sister in next to him, a realization struck him. He smiled sweetly. Sharing the kingdom with a princess, perhaps, would not be so bad after all.

In contrast to her first 45 minutes, India has been a lovely, content little girl, a good little sleeper.

I've tried to get up with her at least half the time for her feedings, but the other morning I found myself alone when Dylan rousted me with a demand for waffles.

"Wha, wha," I mumbled, my morning I.Q. slowly rising like the thermometer on a December day to double digits. "Wha.. where's your mom?" I wondered.

The Redhead, overhearing the conversation on the baby monitor, took my question to mean I was sending Dylan back to her for breakfast. She stormed into the bedroom to give me what-for.

Well, if that's the way she was going to be, to heck with it. I went right back to sleep. An hour later, when I strolled out into the kitchen, she scowled at me.

I offered a sincere apology.

"A lot of good that does now," she responded. Redheads are not noted for their forgiving nature.

She plunked, seething, into her chair, and I sat down on the ottoman looking her in the eye.

"Look, honey, I know I should have gotten up, but you know, when a guy apologizes, you should cut him a little slack. And if you're ever wrong and you decide to say you're sorry, I promise to graciously accept your apology."

The smoke rolling out of her ears began to ebb. She showed a hint of a smile. "I've apologized before," she fibbed defensively.

My eyes brightened. "Oh yes, I remember. The band played. And there was a parade. It was a very big celebration."

When she didn't slug me, I knew the war was over. It was just as well. Just then, India cooed, and The Redhead scrambled for her bottle. And I got up to fix Dylan a waffle.

© Tony Bender, 2000

As Good as It Gets

It's worse. When it gets to "for better or worse" count on the man you marry to be at his worst at all times. That goes for women, too. That way you won't be disappointed.

I think the Redhead and I have an average marriage except for maybe the whips and chains and dungeon thing. When my buddies and I compare marital issues on our annual fishing trip, the issues that frustrate them and their wives are the same.

Now, scientifically, one might deduce from such research that all men are idiots and all women are harpies. Let's just say we are different. Wildly different. I'm not even sure it's a good idea for men and women to live together.

After being admonished for the thousandth time, to please put the dirty dishes in the dishwasher instead of leaving them in the sink, I sighed and did. But I forgot to rinse them before I put them in the dishwasher.

I will go to my grave arguing that it is ridiculous to wash dishes before we put them in a dishwasher. We don't wash our clothes before we put them in the washer, for heaven's sake!

Anyway, an exasperated Redhead bent my ear a bit. She thinks I don't love her when I make a mess. No, I make a mess because I'm occasionally messy. And I would clean it up.

Eventually.

If she didn't always beat me to it.

I cited my good qualities (and let me assure you, it took a very long time) and, frustrated, whined, "If this is my worst sin, how tough would it be to just live with me the way I am? Maybe this is as good as it gets!"

You want to see a woman tremble in fear? Tell her flat out there is no hope you will ever change.

I blame it all on women's magazines. *Glamour. Redbook. Good Housekeeping. Self.* These magazines set women's expectations unrealistically high. (Sort of the way *Playboy* does for men.)

They all feature articles that are pure fiction. "GET YOUR MATE TO HELP AROUND THE HOUSE!" the headline reads. "YOU TOO CAN HAVE A 50-50 MARRIAGE!"

The psychobabble instructions sound like you're trying to housebreak a puppy.

Like that will work.

Part of the problem is misrepresentation. I'll admit, I'm not the same handsome, attentive, witty, thoughtful guy my wife dated.

And when we dated, she never once complained about the ever-present stack of soiled dishes in my kitchen. I know she was thinking, "I'll change just a few things about him and he'll be perfect."

Now she has a man who walks around in his underwear, is increasingly flatulent and still can't figure out the dishwasher. On the other hand, I'm still handsome.

She no longer wakes me with an erotic lick of my ear. Now I am awakened by having a 40-pound four-year-old pouncing on my groin. Or I am roused by four-month-old India at 3 a.m. who isn't hungry. She just wants to sit on my lap and watch *I Love Lucy* reruns.

It's all part of the survival instinct. Children know they must keep their parents up at night to the point of exhaustion and then wake them three hours before sunrise.

This eliminates any possibility of amorous activity and

explains why most people's dungeons are so dusty. And children get all the attention with a minimal chance there will be any more siblings to compete for parental attention.

Then these women's magazines have the audacity to publish sex surveys. The Redhead was citing me the number of times per month the average couple does the wild thing. According to her calculations, we are below average.

"Who could possibly do it that often?" I complained, embarrassed. "Don't they have jobs? Or children? Who did they survey—porn stars and hookers and Charlie Sheen?"

But the truth is, even if they had surveyed monks and vestal virgins, it might be a statistical dead heat the way things are going lately.

So we decided to get away for a long romantic weekend in Deadwood, the Redhead and I. Her folks would wrangle the children. For four long, peaceful days we would relax, eat fine food, sleep in and make good use of the hotel dungeon.

We secured the Bullock Suite at the historic Bullock Hotel which featured historic victorian furniture, an historic, ornate bed the size of Wisconsin, and an historic Jacuzzi.

In the dim light it was very romantic. I held the Redhead's hand and she looked meaningfully into my eyes.

"I miss my kids," she said.

© Tony Bender, 2001

With the bare bulb glaring in my eyes, I was asked all sorts of questions about my health, my family's health, my neighbor Ned's gout... Life insurance companies have no interest in insuring anyone who might actually die.

"Do you smoke?" she asked.

"Only when I'm drunk," I said.

Tony Bender
Life Insurance, 1998

Friends Along the Trail

One fine summer day Rodney and I rewarded Marlene for taking us to Lake Hoskins by filling her Pontiac with live frogs. Dozens of them. She didn't discover them until she was driving us home, which precipitated several interesting lane changes.

We never found all the frogs.

But we assured her we did.

Tony Bender
The Cuz, 1995

"I hear yuh got
an earring!"

"Oh, no!" I blurted loudly like you do sometimes when you read something particularly sad and particularly shocking in the newspaper.

It was lunch time on a Wednesday at the *Ashley Tribune*. I abandoned my chef's salad and peered at the obituary, studying the grinning face in the picture, letting it register that the grin was gone.

The Redhead looked up in alarm from her fajita salad, delicious take-out from Dakota Family Restaurant here in Ashley.

"What!?" she asked. "What!?" she demanded like she does if I sound the alarm when we are driving, and some crazy person tries to kill us on the highway.

"What!?" she will demand as the crisis unfolds, as I swerve to avert disaster or kick the brake.

She always gets angry when I am too flumoxed by the emergency, too tongue-tied, too damn busy trying not to die to answer immediately.

She was frustrated again by my pause, but she waited, fork poised in transit.

I lowered the pages of the *Adams County Record*. "Bert Berg died," I said, still not quite believing that the old veterinarian was gone. I was surprised by my surprise and at a sense of loss that leapt from nowhere.

Somehow I could not believe that Bertram Berg actually could die. He was too big, too much ingrained in my mind where I keep the tickles, the grins and the stories I tell over and over because they make me smile as well as those I tell.

The loss I felt surprised me because sometimes you don't know how much you will miss someone until they are gone.

I tried to explain to The Redhead the loss, but I was explaining to myself as well, I guess, because Bert and I weren't best buddies. Not any more than most folks in a small west river town are. We didn't exchange Christmas cards. Didn't call.

But Bert introduced me to the best dog I ever owned. And I miss Duck Dog, that hard-headed, lovable Brittany, even today.

Bert was good at introductions. He introduced me to Hettinger—to the way things are out in west river country—bigger, more pugnacious, as rugged as the country where the buttes soar with their flat top glacial haircuts.

I was burrowed away in that musty, leaky-roofed building on Hettinger's Main Street that first day in 1991. It was December. I was hiding, still not quite sure what I'd gotten myself into now that I was the publisher of a newspaper less than six months after becoming a newspaperman in the first place.

I knew the truth. I had been hired because they needed a warm body. The paper was headed toward bankruptcy, and you don't need an old salt to steer a sinking ship to the bottom.

I had taken the position in a fit of pique, a month after I turned down the offer in the first place.

I left my job as a reporter in Williston after a spat with the editor, who taught me much about reporting but had much to learn about dealing with people.

"I'm not qualified," I had said the first time I was asked to come to Hettinger. But after the last straw at the *Williston Daily Herald*, I called back. "Let's talk," I said.

That I should be drawn by fate to a community with a similar sense of independence was no coincidence I see now, looking back.

I heard the booming voice in the back, in the dingy, poorly lit office that was mine. I shrank deeper behind my desk as the voice came closer, having successfully maneuvered past Colette at the front desk.

With no choice, I rose from the desk and walked out of the office to meet the voice in the long layout room.

"So you're the new editor!" he said in a timbre bigger than he was, and he was no wimp. He grinned. Lots of teeth. He sidled up around me and peeked at my ear. "I hear yuh got an earring!" he said, grinning some more as he shook my hand. I could not help but notice he was missing one of his ears.

That was my introduction to Hettinger, where your curiosities are discussed to your face as easily as behind your back.

As a community, it was bold. Quarrelsome sometimes, not much given to pretension. I do not know if that was the message Bert intended to deliver that day but I doubt it.

Even so, his hello served notice that this was not a place where the meek shall survive long. This is a place where, hell, if you're going to think it, yuh might as well say it.

It was a lesson learned tolerably well, but I never could completely shake off the decorum of east river ways to ask Bert about that missing ear.

There were many more good times in Hettinger than bad over the next seven years. The paper never did sink. It excelled and still does today. I made fox hole friends, and as much as there is a place in my heart for that town, there is a piece of my heart still there.

That is what I tried to express to The Redhead, failing miserably as I stared at that grin.

And the earring? It fell out one day, six or seven years back, and I never bothered putting it back in.

Guess I didn't need it anymore.

© Tony Bender, 2001

Dick's Bra

I never set foot in Dick's Bra. Never sidled up to the bar on a hot summer day for a cold one. But someday I will.

Dick's Bra has been closed for quite a few years. Five or seven, nobody's quite clear on that. It stands empty in Verona, the basement now a dank swimming pool, a home to salamanders and frogs. But if you listen closely on a quiet night, you can hear echoes of laughter faintly bouncing off the creaking walls. You can hear the clink of glasses being washed and the thud of drafts being emptied by tanned farm boys in sleeveless shirts. Those were the days.

Outside, there's a bullet hole through the "B" in the sign from the night Donny Brandt aimed that "empty" pistol at it. That's the story I get from The Redhead and she should know—a couple generations of Lovgrens rested elbows on that bar and toasted better times.

The pub got its unusual name from the Tamlyn kids—Dick's kids—who were put in charge of lettering the sign. Their puckish sense of humor was never reversed. Dick's Bra it became and Dick's Bra it stayed.

These stories came to me like orphaned children after the actual bar was rescued from the deteriorating building.

When The Redhead and I embarked on our basement remodel, we thought it might be nice to build in a wet bar, but saddled with a restrictive budget, the plan was shelved early.

That's when The Redhead's dad mentioned Dick's Bra. The bar might still be salvageable, he thought. The Redhead loved the idea.

Her dad gave Dick a call. The way it sounded to us, second-hand, was that Dick was kind of honored that we wanted to restore a section of the old bar. Old bartenders can get kinda sentimental that way.

When Uncle Carsten found out we were going to retrieve the bar, he fumed a bit. After all the scraped shins that bar had cost him, hell, it should be his, he fussed.

Seems the local boys, when their athletic prowess had been enhanced and their common sense muted by barley pop, would try to jump, flatfooted from the floor to the top of the bar. Long-legged Carsten never made it. But that never stopped him, LeRoy Schneider and Keith Raatz from trying. There were a lot of blood-ied shins along the way.

The night before The Redhead and her dad went to pick up the bar, Dick went down to polish it up one last time. Even cleaned up, it's not much to look at. It will need refinishing. But it has a soul. It has memories.

Loading the bar would require some muscle, so Brian Rourke was recruited. That's what you get for driving around doing nothing on a Saturday morning in Verona.

Mako was not so easily lured in. As they stood in front of the old bar waving him in like a flagman on a pitching carrier deck, he hollered plaintively from half a block a way, "What do you want?" A suspicious man, that Mako.

But they reeled him in, too.

There was a lone beer bottle resting on the bar in the dingy light. A clean, shiny, modern beer bottle.

Dick claimed not to know how it got there. "Somebody must have come in after I left," he said.

Coulda been the ghosts, I suppose. Haunts like Dick's Bra

have lots of spirits, swaying softly in inebriation, mumbling non-sensical songs, giggling madly.

Yup, coulda been a ghost.

Or it could have been Dick.

One last good-bye.

One for the road.

© Tony Bender, 1998

Getting By

No one ever ran on him. And if word hadn't gotten around—and mostly it had—jaws would drop in the first inning when a white bullet practice throw would whistle over the mound and smack into the shortstop's glove, a foot to the first base side of second.

He was a scamp. Always pushing the rules, pushing the boundaries. His eyes wide, he would grin when the light bulb in his head glowed at the notion of some new mischief.

We were never formally introduced. We just sort of collided. As the oldest of six, I delivered papers for my spending money. He idled away his day, batting golf balls into the tall grass in the pasture behind his house.

I was introduced to his arm as I rode my bike, delivering papers. From his yard, he and his buddy zipped crab apples at me. Some thudded softly off my T-shirt. Others stung and left welts.

He had a gun. An average stick. But behind the plate he had the lazy looseness of a cat. Woe to the runner who strayed too far off first, whose mind wandered for even a moment, hypnotized by the lazy motions, the seductions of nonchalance of the catcher.

It could turn in a split second, the ball a blur as it nearly tore through the immense pocket of the first-bagger's glove whose sweeping tag would prematurely end the runner's stand.

• • •

"Pussies!" I yelled, defiant, at the apple throwers. It was the most terrible insult to a puberty-plagued boy in those days. Such was my anger.

Before I could untangle from by bike, they were on me, 30 copies of GRIT spilling to the ground. He kicked me in my right eye and for weeks the white was an ugly, bloody red. "Pussies!" I screamed, quivering from rage, standing on the steps of my English teacher's home where I had been ambushed.

• • •

My skills were pedestrian. I was a grinder. Average arm. Average speed. Flawed swing. Dangerous glove.

I watched him every day from center field knowing if I had his skills, I could make the majors, and knowing all the same this would be my last year. There would be no college ball after my last Legion season. After my last summer in the centerfield sun, I would be relegated to the pasture, to the uneven fields and short fences of slow pitch.

If I was a pedestrian player, and I was, I had eyes. And I knew a ballplayer when, on those rare occasions, I saw one.

He was charmed, I thought in those days. He must have rolled and crashed a half dozen cars, always stumbling away inebriated and unharmed. Untouchable.

Always his father was there to pay the lawyer. To grease the skids. To appease the law. Because he loved his son—and how could you not? In those days he was lovable in a reckless sort of way.

I wished then my father loved me that much, but all he ever said was, "If you end up in jail, you get yourself out."

He would crouch ever so low, and when Hutch's fastball approached, he would steal it before the bat could connect. Sometimes, the bat would nick the glove, and the batter would complain because it was, after all, interference. But the three-dollar-a-game umpires lacked the polish to catch the larceny.

He had a mouth, and behind the plate it never stopped moving, never stopped spitting insults.

It infuriated the batters and they could not hit. Such was their anger. Some days he pushed so many buttons I feared the benches would clear, and we would have to rescue him from a lynching. But you do not see bench-clearing brawls in American Legion baseball in South Dakota.

Well, one day someone *did* charge the mound when he was pitching with that golden arm. It was in batting practice.

I could live with the drop-off-the table curve though it was better than any we would see in an actual game. But he insisted on throwing knucklers. Infuriating, dancing, impossible-to-hit knuckle balls.

"Cut it out!" I ordered. "When the hell am I going to see a knuckle ball in a game?"

But yet another knuckler danced in. And another. And one more.

"You son of a bitch!" I yelled. I was halfway to the mound, bat in hand, because I was going end his life when he broke into that grin. I couldn't kill him then. You can't kill a man who is grinning at you.

He always seemed to get by. Always played the angles. Always, it seemed, found a way to get an edge on life.

He went to the army to avoid jail and when he didn't like the army, he got kicked out. He got married three times and screwed up three times.

I was his best man at the third, and he promised this time it would be different because he loved her. I almost believed him.

I had seen glimpses of his mortality. I watched as that cannon arm tried time after time to hit the bottom of the water tower with a baseball. But gravity pulls down cannon balls and rifle shots and he could not do it.

He fell short. Miserably short. Booze, cigarettes and worse

took a toll and one day, years after I had charged the mound, we tossed a ball in the shadows of the trees overhanging the street. He grimaced as he threw. His arm was gone.

So was his protector. When his dad died, there was no one to pay the lawyer, to make right the wrongs of a son. When I would return from wherever my career had taken me, he would be there, fresh out of jail, fresh out of yet another scrape.

I would shake my head disapprovingly. He would listen to my lecture and promise to do better, but he never did. And then we would golf and he would trash-talk while I putted, but sometimes I won.

We would talk about baseball sometimes, but it never seemed to bother him that he had wasted his chance the way it ate at me.

I saw him less as we got older and my obligations grew, but I saw him a few weeks ago in an aged green Plymouth. I stopped. He stopped, cigarette dangling from his mouth.

"Got a license?" I asked.

"Yup. Got a job, too," he frowned. He didn't bother telling me that this time things would be different because he knows I stopped believing him years ago.

"Don't screw it up," I said.

He nodded, blew a puff of smoke and contemplated my order. It grew uncomfortably silent except for the rumble of a muffler gone bad.

So we nodded and drove off in opposite directions like always.

I guess he's getting by.

© Tony Bender, 2001

What Friends
Will Do

Dear Jason,

I have written this letter to you a hundred times in my head. That I had not committed it to paper has hung over my head like Damocles' sword.

So why do I sit here this morning finally writing as my children sleep? I cannot explain why this is the moment I must write. All I know is that I could not sleep and it is strange, because I am usually a very good sleeper.

Perhaps it is because India is sleeping fitfully tonight beside me in her crib, that caused me to sit bolt upright and head to my computer. Maybe it has something to do with the crescent moon I saw driving home at 10:30 tonight, almost red and magnificent. It could be the moon, but I don't think it is that. It is the full moon that drives us to do the unusual, that causes the demons to be loosed. So if it is not the demons that have wakened me, perhaps it is the angels or a benevolent spirit guide. Maybe it was just the wind.

This I can not answer.

Other questions you may have are easier but not easy. Like why is it that I think of you so often and worry about you and your parents? Why do I call your lawyer to see how you are doing, to see if you are any closer to being released? Why is it that I feel this strange kinship across the miles and the generations?

Why do I share your sorrow?

It is 2:09 a.m. and now, at last, I will tell you. It is because I know, that had time and circumstance bent the wrong way for me, as it did the night you crashed into Cari Bailey's car, my life would have been thrown into the abyss, as yours has been.

It could have been me.

That it wasn't, I cannot explain. But I will share the lessons learned, the meaning I have found and the hope.

This is a story I have told only to a few.

It was November 26, 1976, the day after Thanksgiving, and I was back from college, ready to celebrate with my friends. My father growled at me that night and told me not to go, and I wonder if he knew... something. I went anyway, because I was invincible. You know the feeling—not anymore—but you remember.

I was driving my first car, a 1967 Pontiac Catalina, 400 cubic inches of V-8 power. I paid $200 for her. We called her the Grey Ghost. Fitting I suppose, because she is a ghost now.

We were drinking beer that night, my four friends and I. There was Gare Bare, Witt, Al Cat and Balowsky, and we were good friends, the kind of friends you just know will be there when things get tough.

Things got tough.

I cannot explain why I pushed the pedal to the floor, sending us screaming through stop signs on a strange road in the fog at 85 mph. I cannot explain anymore than you can explain what you were doing that night 27 years later. Are young men crazy? Suicidal? I only know for sure that we are not bulletproof.

I saw the steep railroad embankment looming out of the fog straight ahead, and I jerked the wheel hard to the left. But no car, no tires, no driver, can make a turn like that at 85.

The bumper clipped off the stop sign on the opposite side of the intersection so cleanly it was suspended for a split-second, straight up in midair. The butt end shattered the glass of the windshield above my head.

So it began, a change in my life's direction so profound I still feel the reverberations today.

I lost my anger that night.

The anger that had me clawing at the world.

The anger that had me screaming sometimes at my parents in frustration, "I did not ask to be here!"

That anger died that night.

And for a moment, so did I.

No moment I have lived is so indelible in my mind as the moment that I died. My memory on this point is pure. Flawless. But it took me years to understand what happened.

Afterward, the change in me was not apparent to those around me. I did not easily change my ways. When you spend your first 18 years trying to cheat life, to work the angles, it is not a habit easily tossed aside. But I changed, just as you have changed.

After the crash, it was silent. Time was suspended and no one moved. The dome light was on, I was convinced of it, because there was a glow from above.

I could see my friends, from above, but they were frozen still. I could not comprehend how I could see 360 degrees around me. I could see Gare Bare and Witt in the front seat and Al Cat and Balowsky in the back. They were hurt. Guilt coursed through me. I had hurt them. Then I saw myself in the driver's seat, slumped to the left, motionless.

Dead.

It is impossible to explain the presence I felt, but I will try, because I was not alone, looking down, seeing full circle, seeing myself, awash in the light that seemed to radiate in every corner and crack of the crumpled Pontiac.

It was time for me to go, the presence gently advised me. My life was a sorry mess, a waste, and the direction I was headed meant sure disaster.

It was time to go.

Time to meditate from other dimensions.

Time to regroup. That is what the gentle presence told me. There were no words, no voice I heard, but the message was there.

"But my friends, I've hurt my friends, and I have to help them," I told the presence. And I did what we all do when things get tough. I promised to change if I could have just one more chance.

The choice to return was mine, the presence allowed. So I came back. Guilt brought me back.

That is how I came to live again. And as I said before, I was not an instant convert. Change came slowly, and even today I struggle to excise the stains on my soul.

But one thing did change in that flash. I lost that deep rage toward the world. For you see, Jason, I had asked to be here after all. Like a petulant child, that realization changed everything. Oh, I still get angry. Indignant. But my anger does not run nearly so deep anymore.

I lost five front teeth that night.

Nearly lost my bottom lip.

Lost my life and got it back.

Left one path and started down another.

My friends all lived. There are stitches and bones that don't work quite right, especially now that we are in our mid forties. But they never resented me for the scars.

When I returned to this dimension, it was bedlam. Gare Bare screamed that the car was going to catch fire, but it did not. I spat blood and teeth, but inside I was serene because I remembered my promise and I remembered where I had been.

The dome light was not on.

Witt, whose cigarette had been pasted to the windshield with blood from a split forehead, went a little crazy. He got into the driver's seat, intending to drive the wreck away, so that I would not get in trouble.

That is what friends do.

It was laughable really. The Grey Ghost was finished. Scrap. Mangled steel. It was the last ride.

I led my friends, bleeding but alive, to the farm house across the road. A county deputy arrived before the ambulance and took Balowsky, Witt and me to the hospital because we looked the worst.

"Who was driving?" the deputy asked. Balowsky made up a story about a transient who had crashed our car and disappeared into the night. That is what he said because he did not want to see me in jail.

That is what friends will do for one another.

Truth be told, the driver who had caused this mess was not the same person who was riding in the front seat, bleeding in puddles on the floor mat.

"I was driving," I said, because I was ready to take my medicine, to begin to atone. Balowsky groaned at my confession and spat blood on the seat from his bleeding lip.

Witt and Balowsky were crazy at the hospital that night. As doctors and nurses hovered over me in concerned huddles, stitching and clamping, Witt burst through the door to see me before being pulled back by the officer.

It looked pretty bad, I know, and he was worried.

Twice more, Witt flew through the swinging doors, each time dragging more officers and orderlies with him, hollering that he wanted to see me before I died.

Silly. I had already died. And I was back.

The third time, I pushed the doctors and nurses away and sat up with stainless steel clamps holding my face together. "Hey, Witt," I said toothlessly, "I'm OK."

He slumped, and the officers in brown and the orderlies in white relaxed their grip. "OK," he said, and walked out.

As I was stitched up, as nurses walked in and out, I could see Witt and Balowsky, flying by in the hall in wheelchairs, popping wheelies, bleeding on the floor, being chased by nurses. I have sometimes wondered about that strange celebration, and I think it was a celebration of our survival.

Witt still carries that scar on his forehead out in Green River, WY, where he's a pretty good coach, and even though I haven't seen him in a while, I know he is still my friend and a damn fine human being.

Balowsky refused to let them shave off that awful wispy mustache he had back then, so they stitched it right into his lip.

Gare Bare and I are still best friends, and through the ups and downs, we have been there for each other, and I don't suppose that will ever change.

Al Cat still has that baby face and the twinkle in his eye when he smiles. I return his smile when I see him, and we remain friends.

A lot of things went terribly wrong that night, but a lot of things went right, too. I still have my friends, and I do not have the scar on my soul I would have if I had killed them.

When my parents got to the hospital, my face was swollen beyond recognition, and my mother laughed, mostly out of relief, I think.

"I told you not to go," my father said.

So Jason, here we are. I am the one who tried to cheat life, the one who broke all the rules and got lucky. You are the one who followed the rules most of the time and then did something stupid and got burned.

It hardly seems fair, does it?

I know that had things gone differently for me, I could not have complained from that other dimension that life was not fair. Because I believe it is. Somehow, some way, in intricacies we cannot understand, life is fair. There are wheels in motion, lifetimes woven with karma, in patterns beyond comprehension.

That does not make the death of Cari Bailey any less tragic. It does not absolve the stain on your soul.

But Jason, I am here to tell you there is hope.

And most certainly, there is light.

I know, because I saw it. Now, because of the light, I do not fear death. And because of the light, I embrace life even more.

If there is light for me, there is certainly light for you.

For all of us.

The debts we have are great in this life, and you may wonder, will sitting in prison serve as payment for your great debt to Cari?

I believe, and you know, it does not. But you must make the best of that time. Don King said when he was in jail, "I didn't serve time. I made time serve me." For all of King's flaws, and they are many, he was right about that.

As long as your mind and heart are not locked up, where you are is not nearly as important as who you are.

Where do you go after you leave those steel bars behind you? You go where your life leads you. And you must trust in the flow. It is when we do not trust in the flow, in the changes in directions, that we suffer the grievous crashes.

Life is a river. Slow and serene sometimes. Swift and frightening at others. But you must go where it takes you. You may fight, but in the end, you will go where the river takes you. It knows where you must be.

You are not the captain.

You are a passenger.

Along the way, you will have opportunities to do good things. Do them for Cari because she would have done good things. Do them because they will help your heart heal.

But don't forget to do good things in your name, too. As much as you have taken away from Cari, I do not believe it would be right for you to give up your whole life.

One life lost is enough.

You will find the way, Jason.

Do not be afraid to find the joy in your journey.

Be strong.

Do not allow others to define you.

Be brave.

71

Know you are loved.

That is what I wanted to tell you.

That is what drove me from my bed on this muggy August night at 2:09 in the morning.

I just wanted you to know I care about what happens to you. I guess that is what friends will do.

—Tony Bender

© Tony Bender, 2001

Writer's note: Jason wrote back and I was moved to tears by the utter sadness and desperation of his letter from the North Dakota State Penitentiary. It was a letter telling of a hard world dictated by animal instinct and brute strength, every day a fight for survival. The depths of Jason's remorse over the death of Cari Bailey are beyond measure. The weight of his conscience continues to punish him far beyond what the penal system can exact. He wants so desperately to reach out to Cari's family but is forbidden. And now I fear we are losing him, too. It was a hard, hard letter to get.

By chance I bumped into Jason's attorney, Tom Dickson, in Bismarck the next week, and I think he summed up the terrible place Jason is at physically and emotionally. "He needs so desperately to be forgiven by Cari's family," he said.

Such a tall order. To forgive will require a grace and compassion rare indeed. And yet, before anyone can move on, before life for the Does and the Baileys can begin again, the anger must be replaced by forgiveness. The awful thing about anger is, as much as it wounds the object of the anger, it devastates the soul from which it rises.

Forgiveness. It is the holiest of gifts and reveals us in that moment to be magnificent. It heals the forgiver and the forgiven. I pray for magnificence. I pray for Cari Bailey and for her family. I pray for Jason. I pray for healing.

I pray, dear Lord, there will be forgiveness.

Werner's Brother

He was a troublemaker. But in my neck of the woods back then, troublemakers were held in high esteem. They still are.

I met him soon after I entered the newspaper business. I was about 10, I suppose, when I began delivering GRIT, a family newspaper, to 32 homes in that town of 400. That was a pretty fair share of the households, but I also ordered 20 extra copies each week which I would hawk on Main Street.

Every week it was a challenge. I learned to overcome objections.

"I can't read."

"There are lots of pictures."

Werner was retired when I met him. Either that or he spent an awful lot of time in town dressed in bib overalls—the blue and white thin-striped Key overalls, with a hand-rolled smoke dangling from his lips.

Years later, those cigarettes would cost him his larynx but not his wit. He would still deliver vocal jabs with a "talker" held close to his neck.

He was short—not as short as Shorty Rush—but by any measure, not a tall man. His face jutted forward, nearly resting on his chest instead of rotating high on his neck, giving him the appearance of a nosy, combative imp. Which he was.

He tortured the folks at the cafe daily, which was high sport among some of the trouble makers, including one stoic old soul who fished about in his oyster stew for a few minutes before calling to the cook, "Does this oyster have a brother?"

Werner's specialty was complaining about the coffee. He knew fresh grounds went in with every pot but complained conspiratorially that the grounds were changed weekly at best.

But he'd paid his nickel, like he did every day for all those years, and that, he thought, gave him the privilege to complain.

Most days the reaction was a sigh. Some days it was a growl. Other days Werner would get run out by an irritated waitress delivering highly uncomplimentary syllables to his ears as he shuffled for cover. And of course, those were the days he lived for. He'd smirk, his eyes would shine, and he would protest the unkind banishment.

Every week I got the same treatment. He'd try to get a rise out of me when I sold him the paper. He couldn't read. He didn't have any money. The price was too high anyway.

But like a pit bull with a pants leg, I dogged him, and every week, moaning and complaining, he went home with a copy of GRIT.

One day, I stopped in the elevator where my dad worked, for a soda, and to unload a few copies to the farmers idling at the counter. There I sold a copy to Werner, and though I don't remember, I'm sure I had to listen to him complain for a good five minutes, as usual, before he gave me the 15 cents. He always bought a paper so I didn't really mind.

When I got uptown, I spotted a couple men outside the butcher shop which also housed a barber shop, and by most accounts, the cutting that was done on either end of the building was professional.

I made my pitch and sold two papers to the three men. The third was Werner Groop. At least I thought it was Werner Groop.

I started to walk away when he challenged, "Hey, aren't you

going to sell me a paper?"

"*I just did. Down at the elevator.*"*(Forgetful old fart.)*

He claimed on a stack of Bibles that I had done no such thing. I squinted up at him, but not too far up, because he wasn't that much taller than me, and just a bit of doubt crept in. The guy I had sold a paper to sure *looked* like Werner and *complained* like Werner.

"That was my twin brother."

I argued that God couldn't be so cruel as to saddle two people with looks like that, for I was a lippy lad, and you had to be to survive the initiations of the troublemakers in my town. The other two guys grinned at this exchange.

The man who looked like Werner demanded I sell him a paper.

And I continued to refuse, much to his delight.

But by God, this was America, a free country, and if a man wanted to buy a paper, he should be able to buy a paper, he groused.

By then, a couple prospective customers stepped out of the Little Store where Gert Prunty sold penny candy to all the kids in town.

Eager to make another pitch, I demanded to see his money. He produced a dime and a nickel. I snatched them before he could change his mind and handed him a paper.

He grumbled that a guy shouldn't have to work so hard to buy a newspaper, and these young whippersnappers don't know the meaning of a nickel and blah, blah, blah.

I cornered a man at the steps of the Little Store.

"*Hey Mister, who is that guy?*"

He looked over my shoulder.

"Werner Groop."

"*He doesn't have a twin brother?*"

"Nope."

The next week I sold Werner a paper on Thursday. He argued not a trifle and seemed quite satisfied with himself.

75

On Saturday, I spotted him in the shade on the bench outside the Ponderosa Bar and tried to sell him my last paper.

"I already bought one," he purred like a cat playing with an about-to-be-eaten mouse.

"But this one's for your brother," I argued.

© Tony Bender, 2000

Ted's Freezer

For days, when Ted Uecker came home, he complained to Nancy that there was an odor in the house. First there was just a hint of a smell. As the days went on, it grew.

Ted's a neat freak and as the week progressed, this was really getting to him. He didn't discover the source until a week later when Nancy was on a rodeo road trip with their daughter Heidi, a barrel racer. By then, the smell had gotten strong enough that Ted could trace it to the prehistoric freezer in the basement.

If this had been a B horror movie, the audience would scream, "Don't open the door!" But folks always walk like lambs to the slaughter into the creepy attic or cellar of doom.

Like there is some immutable cinematic law, curiosity overwhelms their will to live and they open the door and Ted did, too.

A week's worth of rotting fish and beef nearly knocked him over and sent him scrambling and retching back up the steps. This was a stink of epic proportions. Neighborhood skunks sought new addresses. The pig farmer down the road called to complain.

It was revoltingly bad.

So Ted did what any man would do.

He called his wife.

Demanded she come right home and take care of this disaster.

Nancy had him call Harriet.

What are friends for?

"Ted, we have got to get this freezer out of here," Harriet said.

No small task. This was an old freezer from the era when they made them out of recycled Sherman tanks. Only heavier.

So Harriet raced uptown to gather help. She found a handful of strapping young men and told them it was an emergency.

Big stink up at the Uecker house.

"Take a whiff boys," Ted told the gagging troops as they descended the stairs, "That's what a five dollar hooker on Hennepin Avenue smells like."

Thus inspired, they hauled the freezer out.

The next day, Harriet went over to check on Ted. The house smelled a whole lot better. Ted had even sliced out the carpet where the freezer had stood.

I'm assuming the landfill accepted the freezer. But just to be on the safe side, if you see a freezer for sale in the classifieds in Hettinger, don't call.

© Tony Bender, 1999

Writer's note: One July 4, when the wind was whipping north of Hettinger, Ted tried to burn the town down with his annual family fireworks extravaganza at Uecker Yards. (He's a cattle buyer.) A rocket started the grass at the nearby airport on fire and while Ted cackled like Nero, Jimmy Howe and I and a couple of others desperately beat on the flames with our jackets. It could have taken out the whole town.

Ted makes Mrs. O'Leary's cow look like a rank amateur.

We barely got it out.

The next morning, each of us showed up at Carmel's Cleaners with eyebrows singed off to drop off the smokey charred remains of our jackets. I was the third jacket in the next day and Carmel raised his eyebrows but didn't bother to ask.

He knows we're friends of Ted Uecker's.

Sportsmen

Setting up the tent is another Three Stooges affair. Bob and Tom usually handle the chore with the manual dexterity of drunken clams.

Tony Bender
Camping with Bureaucrats, 1996

Gone Fishin'

They get surly. Every year at this time our wives get surly, and that's how we know it is time for our annual pilgrimage to the mountains, the continental divide of the Colorado Rockies.

When we arrived at Taylor Lake, after the tent was pitched, I laid down the law. We would have to call home. Every day. Last year, no one called. Not once. "Whose idea was that?" I railed, remembering the coldest of cold shoulders when I got home. "Were we nuts?"

So I called. I told The Redhead how hard it was raining, how awful the fishing was, how much I missed her and the kids and how eager I was to get out of this living hell and back home to her.

"Think she bought it?" Booker asked after I hung up the pay phone.

"Naw," I said.

It's not about the fishing. If it was, we would be miserable, Booker, Tom and I, because we are poor fishermen at our best and pitiful at our worst. We are the poster children for PETA, because around us, the fish are safe.

It has become a tradition, this trip, a renewal of old friendships. A chance to tell new stories about the different paths we have taken through life, and a chance to tell old tales around the campfire, even as the evening temperature drops to freezing up here where the tree line ends, where the pines just throw up their hands and refuse to go on.

Each year there are new adventures, but there are constants, too. The mountains remain immense, purple and spectacular. The stream gurgles and foams beside our tent and once in a while a fly fisherman will artfully work his lasso up the stream past us, delicately dancing against the current and over the slick rocks.

Each year Tom fumbles with line so tangled Harry Houdini would be stumped, while Bob and I drag bait past schools of indifferent rainbows.

And each year we huddle to divvy up the expenses like old ladies working a three dollar check for coffee and pie at the local cafe.

When the glove compartment jammed impenetrably shut with their wallets inside, Booker and Tom believed it was a miracle, a sign from above that I would fund this year's excursion.

I believe the Lord helps those who help themselves. I pried. I wedged. I broke the handle. It held up like a Wells Fargo truck. I was reaching for the cutting torch when Tom suggested we remove the screws on the hinge using the wire cutter, lying lonely in my tool box. He was on the second screw when he cursed, bled and rushed into the marina.

"I have some bad news and some good news," he said when he returned. "The bad news is, I just amputated my index finger."

82

"What's the good news?" Bob wondered.

"I think it will make good bait," Tom said.

There are constants. Each year my friends set new records for flatulence. This year I took charge of the menu. Fresh fruits and vegetables. No baked beans. And still they were prodigious, visibly depleting the ozone layer at our towering altitude and collapsing my left lung.

As we drove to the pond creatively named Pothole #2, where browns would ignore us like gorgeous girls at a nightclub, I heard a familiar rumble from Tom's seat.

I rolled down the window and began to crawl out at 35 mph.

"It doesn't stink," Tom assured me.

"I can't afford to take a chance with my good lung," I said.

At the campfire that night, we swilled Hornito's and told ghost stories that were completely true except for the parts that weren't.

By midnight I had the chills, and I couldn't tell for sure if it was because of the foreboding tales or the ominous weather brewing over our heads.

Lightning lit up the tent like a 100 watt bulb. Wind gripped the fabric and shook it like a rottweiler with an ankle as we burrowed into dampened sleeping bags.

I must have fallen asleep, I figured, as the storm raged. How else could Bob have gotten by me with our only flashlight as I slept by the door?

A light glowed eerily from outside against the tent wall as the wind howled. "What's with the light?" I mumbled sleepily.

Bob and Tom sat bolt upright when they realized the light flickering outside was not my doing.

We all knew, instinctively, that anyone one outside our tent in that remote location, at that hour, in weather only Bella Lugosi could appreciate, could only be some sort of madman.

"We're all gonna die!" I screamed as I flung open the tent flap to meet my murderer.

A tattered tarp flapped in the hurricane, anchored by one

tent stake, thunder rumbled and my heart stopped as I saw the light. One charred log, leaning tall against the stones of the fire ring, glowed and flickered as the blast of air rushed past, stirring it to new life.

We would live.

I tiptoed barefoot around the cold swampy camp in the storm, recovering items headed for New Mexico, before settling down on my air mattress. Nervous chuckles were the last thing I heard before I slept.

Twenty hours on the road and two days later I was home. Dylan met me at the stairs and jumped into my arms with a hug that crushed a vertebrae.

India spotted me and grinned in adoration and The Redhead smiled as I kissed her.

"How was the trip?" she asked.

"Awful," I said. "Just awful. Couldn't have been worse."

"But I'm sure you'll do it all again next summer."

"Well, the boys are counting on me," I said.

© Tony Bender, 2001

Mickey's Ball

I suppose I dug around in the closet for 20 minutes or so after I heard the news. But closets do not easily abandon their games of hide and seek.

I know it's there—I'm sure it's in there. It's hard to explain why I felt the need to hold it at that moment. I guess it's the connection to things past.

He was already a legend when I was born. But his retirement in 1968 was lost among the falling giants—Martin Luther King and Bobby Kennedy. It was a bad time for heroes.

Fifteen years before, he could run like the wind, and he covered center field for the Yankees like a human vacuum.

Statistically, Willie Mays was better. Duke Snider? Well, hell, he was The Duke of Flatbush. But Mickey Mantle was magic. After all, here was the man who inherited center field from the

Yankee Clipper.

Inherit, perhaps, is the wrong word. It suggests something not earned. Ascension is probably closer. Amazing. DiMaggio retires, and Mantle steps up. In the religion that is baseball, it was like replacing Buddha with Jesus.

Legions of young men followed every box score, every broadcast. Mickey Mantle was, very simply, the best baseball player ever.

Still, the hallowed records don't bear that out. He finished 200 homers behind Aaron. Never stole as many bases as Rickey Henderson. Never came close to Pete Rose's total hits, and he finished his career batting under .300. But he could have done every one of those things. He just decided, inexplicably in the back of his mind, not to.

You see, baseball was still a game then, and Mickey Mantle played. It wasn't about records for him. Mickey, as high priest of baseball, was a blasphemer and a bit of an agnostic.

I remember my Uncle Norbert telling me about seeing Mickey in center field, carrying on with the fans.

"Hey, Mick, what'd ya do last night?" they'd ask.

Mick would grin and tilt his head back, his fist imitating a bottle, and he'd guzzle an imaginary longneck in center field for the fans.

Norbert laughed, his eyes twinkling behind his glasses, when he told the story. We lost Norbert a few years back when his liver finally gave up.

I suppose the story shouldn't be funny anymore, but it is. To hell with the sanctimonious, politically correct hand-wringing about Mantle's battle with alcoholism.

Who are we to question the choices of an immortal as we live in our safe world, measuring each risk and tiptoeing around danger? Mickey Mantle lived, and he inspired millions. Let that be enough.

My father was one of those infatuated with the legend of Mickey Mantle. He often mourned the loss of Mantle's rookie card—a victim of Grandma's housecleaning obsession, I imagine.

Several years ago, I got my hands on a ball signed by The Mick. It was akin to having the Holy Grail.

Dad was thrilled when I gave it to him. He kept the ball in his trophy case, right above his treasured collection of shot glasses.

I don't think there was a time when I visited that I didn't peer into the case just to see that ball. A couple of years ago, I got the ball back by default. Inherited it.

But you know how it is when you move. Things get packed away and stay packed for years. They aren't things you need, really, but there are memories inside the clutter of the musty cardboard.

When The Mick's life ended, I braved the closet, looking for the ball. I should have rented a bloodhound.

But I know that ball is in there.

Just like I know out of the corner of my eye I'm going to see my father dozing on the couch next time I'm home. Just like I'm sure Mickey Mantle is still roaming center field in Yankee Stadium, clowning for the fans and making Casey Stengel smile.

© Tony Bender, 1995

Writer's note: I eventually did find the ball. It is carefully tucked away on display behind glass in Dylan's room. He does not yet know what it means, but someday he will.

This You Do
For Yourself

If you're lucky, you'll have one teacher or one coach who will touch you, inspire you; someone who will change the direction of your life.

As children, we don't recognize how subtle they are, the forces that steer us. Like the flap of a butterfly's wings may redirect a jet stream, so too, can the right comment at the right time from the right person gently grasp the soul of the listening ears.

I had both. The coach and the teacher. And they speak to me every day. Mrs. Rollo, my English teacher, will not remember the moment she reached me. But with particular praise of a composition she led me to believe that I could be, no, that I *was*, something special. I cannot say if that is so, but she allowed me to believe it.

Perhaps, because I was blessed with inspirations, I am able to see more clearly when the connection is made around me. I saw it in Hettinger when a banty rooster of a coach, Randy Burwick, directed a team to the state wrestling title a couple years ago. Still, like a sorcerer's secrets, his remain a mystery to me. I see the optimism, the encouragement, but I cannot fathom what hold he has that drives otherwise underachievers to greatness, to the realization that one must not be defined by others but by one's self. But I see the look in his wrestlers' eyes. He has

88

taught them to wage a crusade. And the crusade will not end.

In Ashley, there's another coach, Gary Hoffman, totally different, equally inspirational. I've seen coaches manipulate minds, looking for an edge, a way to connect, a way to exact performance. Hoffman is different. He believes, lives and breathes what he says.

A young wrestler remarked to him once at a varsity wrestling meet, "There sure aren't many people here."

"Remember that," he told the boy. "That's life. When you get home after a hard day on the job, there won't be 300 people there to console you. And when you have a good day, there won't be 300 people to applaud you."

The message is clear.

This you do for yourself.

As these coaches and teachers reach out and touch these young men and women, so must have they been touched by their coaches and teachers. Inspiration does not manifest itself like some New Testament miracle. It is a seed. It must be planted, watered occasionally and granted room to find the sun. And from the bloom, the seeds scatter, occasionally to fertile ground.

Hoffman, a farmer, sees ever so clearly the parallels. He demands respect for the generations who came before. "When you get home tonight," he tells his team after a pounding in the wrestling room, "you may want to have more to eat."

Then you must remember your grandfathers and great-grandfathers who came to this prairie with nothing, he says. The ones who plowed behind draft horses and oxen. The ones who threshed in the hot sun. Many times they, too, came home to meager rations.

Great were their sacrifices.

That is the blood that courses through your veins, Hoffman tells them. Good solid German blood. "And somewhere, your ancestors are watching and they know your sacrifices and they are proud."

The message is clear.

This you do for your ancestors.

In this life, you must not shame those who built this place, who built you.

Hoffman believes this.

Because it is true.

I envy Hoffman's wrestlers.

And Burwick's.

For I am on the outside, looking in.

© Tony Bender, 1998

The Race

When I found out Gus was ill, I asked for his address so I
could write. But a week later he was gone. Gus was
always too fast for me...

●●●

It was on the church steps that the bet was made—though it
didn't seem blasphemous at the time.

Gus was needling me about my sister's skill as a centerfielder for one of the three women's teams in the community.

Heck, she'd learned the game from me. She should have
been good after playing years of hardball with the master.

I was playing centerfield for one of the teenage teams in town
and we were good. And me, I'd yet to commit an error, and I was
pounding the ball pretty good, I reminded Gus.

"Well and good," said Gus, "but for my money, Sherry is the
best centerfielder in town. Bar none."

And then he threw in the topper. "I'll bet she's faster, too."

Well, a man can take only so much. That, I knew, was just
not true. Back in those days, I had pretty fair wheels. I scoffed
at the notion. My sister, faster than me? Give it a rest, Gus!

The hook was set. So dollars were passed to an intermedi-
ary—Frederick didn't have a bookie—and a few side bets were
cast. I was confident enough to take all bets.

Fifteen minutes later, a small crowd had gathered at the baseball field, and Gus continued to ride me. I couldn't wait to take his money.

But he got a little nervous when I started lacing up my spikes. "Hey, no spikes," Gus whined.

I argued, but sentiment was with Gus and Sherry. I knew I'd be slipping on the outfield grass since I was about 50 pounds heavier, but I figured I could spot her a few yards and still win. So I acquiesced.

We started at the centerfield fence, and sure enough, Sherry had a good 20 yards on me before I got going in the slick grass. But I passed her at pitcher's mound, just 60 feet from home plate and victory.

I would have loved to have seen the look on Gus' face.

But somehow, Sherry found another gear. And when we crossed home plate, she was ahead by a nose.

Oh man, Gus was in his glory. He hooted. He heckled and he collected. I never lived it down. Gus wouldn't let me.

That was Gus.

We never had a rematch. Some things are best left just as they are. Sherry was faster. But no one was faster than Gus.

The thing about Gus was he could beat you and make you like it even as he crowed like a rooster.

•••

I have no doubt that even as I write, Gus is taking St. Peter's money on some sucker's bet. I know he is in heaven. Anyone who can gamble on the church steps and get away with it must be in good with the Lord.

I didn't get to talk with him one last time, but Gus left me with a pretty good story to tell.

There is a little less mischief in the world today.

And I for one am going to miss it.

© Tony Bender, 1996

Big Daddy

Since I usually drop off Dylan at daycare, I get daily updates:

"You might want to keep an eye on him. He's started flushing things down the toilet."

"Like what?"

"A Volkswagen and our dog."

I was impressed. That dog of theirs is really big.

"So how's the dog?"

"Fine, but since we fished him out of the septic tank, he can't come in the house anymore."

I know where this is leading. My daycare lady is thinking she deserves more money—combat pay. But a deal is a deal.

Tony Bender
Boy Genius, 1998

The Great and Mighty Da-Da

"So how is the baby doing?" the bank teller asked.

"Well," I began as the other two tellers sidled in from the left and right to hear the latest adventures of Little India. "She's been a little bit under the weather..."

Heads nodded sympathetically. "So that means she spends even more time on my lap."

Smiles brightened. "She must really love her daddy," one offered.

"Oh, she does," I replied. "But she *really* loves her brother. Dylan can make her laugh, and she watches every movement he makes. And frankly, I resent it. He doesn't feed her, change her or bathe her."

There were a couple understanding titters.

"And she *really* loves her mom. She can make her laugh, too. I guess I'm just good for sitting."

The tellers laughed and returned to their stations.

But things between India and me are coming along just fine. During her bath yesterday, Indy sputtered with joy as I pretended to eat her toes. It wasn't the unbridled laughter Dylan or The Redhead can elicit, but it was laughter just the same.

And our little six-month-old has been chattering quite a bit

95

lately and her favorite word is Da Da. I heard her say it clear as a bell as she sat on my lap the other evening. The Redhead, fixing supper in the kitchen, heard it too.

Then she said it again. And again. I repeated it to her. "Da Da." And she said it right back as I grinned at her.

"Atta girl!" I crowed. "That's right. I'm your Da Da!"

"Oh she doesn't know what she's saying," The Redhead hurrumphed jealously.

"Aww c'mon. She does too know what she's saying," I argued hopefully.

"Then why does she always say Da Da to me?" the spoilsport in the kitchen asked.

"Because she wants *me*," I sniffed.

"Yeah, yeah," The Redhead muttered, vexed. She always says "yeah, yeah" when she knows she has lost the argument.

Indy and I sat in the easy chair and rubbed it in all night chanting "Da Da."

We had lots of time.

"Who is very handsome?"

"Da Da!"

"Who is the smartest daddy around?"

"Da Da!"

"Who do you love the best, Indy?"

"Da Da!"

By 8 p.m., after I had tucked Dylan in, and Mom had followed up with a "special good-night kiss," The Redhead retired to the bedroom.

I stayed up with Indy. Even if she dozes off, I try to wake her around 10 p.m. for a final feeding, thereby increasing the chances she will sleep through.

If she does get up in the middle of the night, The Redhead gets up with her. And she usually gets up with Indy when she rouses at a punctual 5:50 a.m. every day.

I was exhausted after our Da Da Fest and thankfully, Indy was too. She slept through.

I heard her at precisely 5:50 a.m. "DA DA!" she cooed loudly. I cringed and pulled the covers over my ears.

"DA DA!"

"No, no honey," I whispered urgently. "It's Ma Ma!"

"DA DA," Indy insisted.

"No, no, I protested. When it's morning, you ask for Ma Ma!"

Indy smiled understandingly through the bars of her crib. "DA DA," she agreed at a decibel level far too high to maintain any reasonable level of secrecy.

"Hey, Da Da," The Redhead purred maliciously, "somebody is calling you."

"Aww, she doesn't even know what she's saying," I said, willing to trade humiliation for 20 minutes more in the sack.

"Oh, I...think...she...does!" The Redhead said, punctuating each word triumphantly.

Sighing heavily, I got up and reached for my robe. I always sigh heavily when I know I have lost the argument.

India grinned up at me as I lifted her from the crib. "Da Da," she greeted.

"Yeah, yeah," I moaned sleepily, stumbling to the kitchen to warm a bottle and start the coffee.

© Tony Bender, 2001

No Ordinary Project

The whole sorry incident took place at one of our favorite restaurants in Rapid City. It's a little Chinese place we used to go to BC (before children). But Dylan has gotten to the point where he's fairly civilized at meal time. As always, the food was delicious and the service was polite and fast. We had won tons, egg-drop soup and lots of rice.

Dylan liked the won-tons, rejected the soup and loved the rice. He managed to charm the waitress despite the growing mess he was making. At home, we have a dog to vacuum up loose specks of food.

Toward the end of our meal, Dylan began grunting loudly like a Samurai warrior. Ohh, oh. This would mean a diaper change. As red as his face was getting, and by the way he was clenching his hands together, I should have guessed that this was no ordinary project.

As we finished up, The Redhead excused herself, and I told her we'd meet her at the vehicle after I paid. I even volunteered, oblivious to the impending carnage, to change the diaper. When I picked him up, the odor nearly felled me. Put him in a small room and you could kill canaries and small mammals with that stuff. Dylan smiled, not at all self-conscious. As I held him, my hand slipped up the back of his shirt where it encountered...a bad thing. So here I am, holding the world's stinkiest child in one hygienically-challenged hand, trying to pay the bill without creating too much of a spectacle.

I wanted to get out of there a quickly as possible—if I didn't get some fresh air I was going to lose it. The manager at the till pretended not to notice the stench. Either that, or his olfactory nerves were quickly and mercifully destroyed.

I signed the ticket with my good hand and sprinted for the Blazer. Since we had parked beside the window, I hated to change him on the tailgate, but no way could I put him in his car seat like that. There was no changing table in the restaurant bathroom.

By this time The Redhead arrived. I was turning green around the gills. We decided to tag team the project.

She got a change of clothes out for Dylan, and I began to wipe him down, holding him, squirming and stinking, by the ankles. The Redhead grabbed a fresh diaper.

Suddenly I was overcome; I couldn't take it. The Redhead grabbed Dylan as I bent over and began calling dinosaurs beside some poor guy's Chevy pickup.

The Redhead giggled uncontrollably at my plight because she is cruel and unusual. When I was done, I went back to help. I pulled the diaper off and as further proof of my insanity, morbid curiosity forced me to look inside.

I started to heave again. So off I went to call more dinosaurs.

All that right in front of the restaurant window.

Well, I couldn't just leave the parking lot like that. I didn't figure it would be good for business. Reluctantly, I went back inside. The manager was oblivious to what had taken place.

"Excuse me, I'm terribly embarrassed..."

He listened politely.

"You know my son..."

He nodded.

"Uh, he filled his pants..."

Another nod.

99

"Well, I was changing his diaper in the parking lot, and I threw up. Twice."

He stared at me.

"Well, it was pretty bad," I finished lamely. "Really, the food was delicious..."

I asked for a bucket of water but he assured me he'd handle it. So I dragged my humiliated self back outside where The Redhead was laughing so hard she had tears streaking her cheeks.

"Funny thing about Chinese food," she said predictably, like it was the funniest thing she had ever heard, "It doesn't stick with you very long!"

© Tony Bender, 1997

Not My Boy

The reports from daycare were unsettling. Dylan was helpful, charming and always took his afternoon nap without a fuss. Visiting mothers commented to me that our boy was "sooo polite." He even asks to be excused from the table—quite a feat for a boy not yet two, they marveled.

"That's not my boy," I always answered confidently. My boy refuses to nap, throws green beans at the dog and has a budding chocolate milk addiction.

Then the other afternoon, I came to pick up Dylan and my suspicions were confirmed. I was a few minutes early and when I walked in, this boy—*this imposter*—was actually picking up his toys and putting them in the toy box.

I went postal. "What have you done with my boy!?" I wailed. Oblivious, Sheila thanked the lad for his help.

"You're welcome," said the boy, who did have a remarkable resemblance to the terror who unfolds clothes as fast as his mother folds them.

"OK, kid," I said, waving him over for the interrogation, "What's your Social Security number?"

"Daddy'" he yelled, ignoring the question, and trotted over to give me a hug. "Not so fast, stranger," I continued. "What's your mother's maiden name?"

101

"Rain, rain, go away, Come again some other day," he sang.
Obviously some alien code.

"Bye," he said to everyone as I carted him out. He said "Bye, bye" to the dog and "Bye, bye" to the car in the driveway. A very polite boy, so you can't blame me, really, for taking him home.

But this is not my boy, I tell you.

This boy can also climb out of the crib in the morning... or the evening if he decides it's not quite bedtime. My boy used to wait patiently in the mornmg for me to grab that extra forty winks. This boy barges into our room, steals my pillow and grabs the remote control to tune in Sesame Street.

The other night, when The Redhead put the boy to bed, I could hear them call to each other:

"I love you Dylan!"

"I love you Mommy!"

It was all very Waltonesque.

But he didn't go to sleep for quite some time. He talked back to the radio. Carried on conversations with his stuffed bedmates.

"You have to peek in there," The Redhead told me.

So I did. He saw me walk in and grinned beatifically from his pillow. Gotcha! I smiled back. I couldn't help it.

"I love you, Dylan," I told him softly, then turned to walk out.

"I love you, Daddy," he said in that sweet, high voice.

And I melted.

That's my boy, you know.

© Tony Bender, 1998

In Stitches

The Redhead streaked out of the office like her skirt was ablaze after the phone call.

"Dylan's up at the hospital. He needs stitches!"

So I called daycare. Turned out Dylan had gashed his knee. Yawn.

I got the gory details later when I got home. Dylan was already crawling on the wounded limb.

"Four whole stitches," The Redhead told me.

Yawn.

"And I have no idea if he got a tetanus shot..."

Yawn.

"Tony, aren't you worried!? He's your son!"

"Look Honey," I responded. "If that kid makes it to 18 without anymore stitches, call the bishop because it will be a miracle."

After supper I showed Dylan all my favorite scars.

"Scars are cool," I told him, beating my chest like an ape. "Arggggh!"

Dylan was mortified. "Dad, will I have a scar?"

"Sure," I said proudly.

"Absolutely not!" The Redhead interjected, a butter knife menacingly pointed in my direction.

"What are you doing?" she asked after Dylan had sauntered back to check on Scooby and Shaggy.

"Telling the truth," I responded.

"Well, stop it!" she said.

© Tony Bender, 2000

School Day

Floyd Tschetter came to get him at 6:40 a.m. Karma danced circles around the school bus with flashing lights in the gloaming. She skipped, tongue lolling, dangerously past the wheels.

Dylan stepped down from the deck to admonish Floyd. "Don't run over my dog!" Karma, a frenetic springer, is alternately a good friend or an irritant to the boy, depending on his mood.

The fog was thick. The sun was still buried behind the Forbes Hills to the east.

The Redhead stood with our five-year-old as the bus crept to a stop. I watched from the door in my bathrobe as India picked at her breakfast beside me.

If the fog was thick, so was my throat as I pictured in my mind the boy that was me in the black and white photo wearing a button down collar, notebook and pencils in hand. That was 38 years ago, and now I finally understood a hint of what my mother felt. Only a hint, mind you. For I am a father and mothers have more exclusive claim to such moments.

The Redhead had fretted for months before kindergarten started because now she would not be there when he faces his first bully. She fretted because he insisted on riding the bus. Alone. At his age.

We didn't talk about it much before the day came. But that first morning she sang a song, "It's a milestone day," as Dylan got dressed. He rolled his eyes—good practice for when he is a teenager and we become even larger embarrassments to him.

As I watched them walk in the fog to the bus in the fog, in the glow of the mist, I could see the poetry of the moment.

The door of the bus hissed open and Dylan jumped in, backpack on. Karma followed only to be banished three steps into the adventure. She will not go to school. She knows all she will ever know.

He was the first on the route. The boy sat three rows back behind Floyd, his tow head barely visible from my view.

And then they were gone.

The Redhead returned to the table to feed India the last spoons full of cereal.

I searched my wife's eyes but she would not look up because if she did, she would cry. Finally, she looked at me. She smiled and she cried.

"He looked so little on that bus!" She smiled some more, but it was a sad sort of smile. A smile reserved for those moments when things change. When those you love start to stretch the tether. Practice for when they finally break away.

"Do you remember..." I said, and I talked about that day in December when she returned home from a business trip to Sturgis with a teddy bear for me. In the bear's hand was an early pregnancy test. It had turned pink and everything changed.

A wave of joy had doused me and left me shaking, leaning against the kitchen counter as I tried to process the news.

She was calm. Peaceful and wiser now, a transformation that comes with motherhood. A confidence and a knowing. And I think, at moments like that, a mother's heart grows to twice the size of a mortal's.

I listed my memories, soothingly but haltingly, surprised that I, too, would feel whatever it was that we were feeling.

India looked at me worshipfully while I spoke, like she always does, her eyes widening with that surprised look she gets with each new experience.

"I remember," The Redhead said before I could finish. She stopped me because in those tender moments it is easy for drips and drops of tears to become puddles.

"That was so long ago!" she said finally, eyes brimming, smiling, pouting because things can never remain the same in this life.

The moments in this life when hearts and souls embrace are so rare. We are always out of step. One heart reaching out. Another shutting down and even in a crowd in this life, we are very much alone. We enter this life alone. We leave it alone. And in between, much more than we should be, we are alone.

That is the lament. As children begin to reach beyond their mother's embrace, as they must, the connections and the embraces decline. This life is lonely. A mother's tears are justified.

© Tony Bender, 2001

Exit Charles

C harles Schultz knew how to make an exit. The day before his final Peanuts comic strip was published, he died.

I didn't know that when I drove the 12 miles to town to get the Sunday paper, but on the way back I heard the news. I had hoped in the final panels of the strip Lucy would finally let Charlie Brown kick the football. But in 50 years that world never changed. Every year good old Charlie Brown trusted Lucy, and every year she let him down.

Gosh, even in my world, the ball sails through the uprights once in a while.

That was the beauty of Charles Shultz' sanguine universe. Winners were always winners. Losers were always losers.

On Valentine's Day, Charlie Brown always got a rock. The Great Pumpkin was never spotted. And Charlie Brown never had a 1-2-3 inning. In spite of it all, Charlie Brown never stopped trying.

Grownups were incomprehensible like all adults are to children, every word from them spewing forth like muted trumpets, WAH WAHH WAHHH WAH WAH.

Over the years, I graduated from Peanuts and Beetle Bailey to Doonsbury and the Far Side, but periodically I checked back in on Peanuts.

You know why? Because they were nice. And predictable.

Lucy offered jaded advice for just a nickel. Schroeder still produced the majestic notes of Beethoven on a toy piano. Linus could not be parted from his blanket, and Pigpen attracted dirt the way trees attracted Charlie Brown's kites.

Snoopy continued to amaze. He flew a doghouse with magnificent skill. He could use a typewriter, too. It was always a dark and stormy night. And he could out-glower any vulture on the block.

I don't imagine it was a cosmic coincidence that Dylan chose the only Charlie Brown book we have on the last day of Charles Schultz' life.

The routine has gotten quite elaborate.

A Flintstones vitamin.

A glass of water. His favorite blue blankie.

His yellow stuffed beaver.

And a book. Sometimes it's Power Rangers. Peter Pan. Fairy tales. The Cat in the Hat. This night he chose *A Charlie Brown Halloween.*

I don't have any excuses really. It might have been a little past his bedtime. Maybe I was a little more tired than usual. But like I do on such occasions, I skipped entire sentences to get through the book faster.

Sometimes Dylan catches me cheating and chides me gently with a disappointed, "Heyyyyy!"

I wish he would have busted me this time. It's a good story. There's a costume contest, and Lucy figures with her great beauty she will win. To make sure, she dictates an edict that Snoopy cannot be a WWI flying ace again because that is the costume that always wins.

Charlie Brown comes as a clown. Linus is a cowboy and Snoopy, who cannot come up with any costume at all, still wins for his amazing resemblance to a beagle.

"Argggh!" says Lucy.

Dylan loved the happy ending and he snuggled into bed and

giggled after my nightly admonition to "sleep tight and don't let the bedbugs bite."

He only broke parole once to give his Mom a big hug and a kiss good night.

It could have been perfect if only I had read all the words.

Good grief!

© Tony Bender, 2000

Politics as Unusual

Back in the Sixties, physicist William Shockley thought it would be a good idea to have people with IQs below 100 sterilized. Congress thought it was a terrific idea. Until they got their test scores back.

Tony Bender
*Great Minds,*1999

Super-heated
Trucker Pee

We're not necessarily proud of it, but North Dakota is number one in urine. Not just horse urine, but according to the Associated Press, North Dakota now leads the nation in exploding human urine.

The state Department of Transportation reports that equipment operators who mow ditches regularly encounter jugs of fermented urine with mower blades.

It's not a good thing.

After baking in the sun for days, theses jugs explode like "little bombs," says one employee who was showered with the stuff twice last year. As one can imagine, no matter how much Old Spice a guy splashes on in the morning, it's pretty tough to pick up chicks over lunch break after an episode like that.

Authorities blame truckers. This can't be safe. Imagine, the next time you have an 18-wheeler bearing down on you, that he doesn't have both hands on the wheel. You have to figure that more than one driver has died with Dave Dudley on the stereo and a funnel permanently affixed to his groin.

Fortunately, the North Dakota Legislature, which specializes in urine laws, may come to the rescue. In the last session, the legislature passed a bill that made it illegal for columnists to unfairly malign horse urine, which I personally feel is superior to

113

most any other animal urine.

Horse urine farmers, a proud and noble lot, were also riled up about criticism from PETA, the People for the Ethical Treatment of Animals. Seems these PETA people felt all this urinating couldn't be good for these horses. Now they have an injunction which means until this whole thing is settled, the horses are going to have to hold it.

This latest urine controversy has lawyers in a tizzy. Does the Urine Slander Act apply to people urine? You would think so. After all, should horse urine be afforded greater protection under the law than actual human waste? So at this juncture, one must be careful about criticizing exploding super-heated trucker pee, which I feel has a delicate yet pungent consistency, not at all dissimilar to fine equine urine.

Lawmakers are considering a Department of Transportation proposal to raise the penalty for subversive urination from $20 to $500. This all comes too late for one state employee, who was drenched in urine twice last year while mowing east of Minot, the unofficial Urine Capital of North Dakota. In one stretch, just a few miles from a rest stop near Minot, this employee once counted 13 containers of urine. That's impressive. Many government employees can't count past ten.

While doctors say urine showers are not harmful (indeed, it can give your hair a lovely sheen), The Minot ditch mower is not so sure. "I've been skunked before and I'd rather have that than this," he said.

© Tony Bender, 1999

Official Speak

You need a translator.

You have to have a translator to understand anyone in an official capacity today.

Once they become officials, like a super hero is bestowed amazing powers, officials receive the transcendent ability to speak in a whole new confusing language—Official Speak.

Thankfully, there is another super hero out there to combat this evil of double speak and misdirection—super reporter Will Gittothepoint. Here's a transcript of Will at work.

•••

The first stop was at the site of the big explosion and fire in a Baltimore tunnel that shut down traffic for several days. There the fire chief described for the cameras what happened.

"Conditions were extremely adverse so we retreated."

You mean you made a run for it.

"Exactly. And then we took a defensive posture."

You stood back and let the fire burn itself out?

"You might say that."

Chief Orwell, afterward what did you find in the tunnel?

"After 72 hours, it became apparent that we could proceed in a prudent manner to the site of the conflagration. Once on the scene, we were able to discern with unqualified certainty that all

115

materials located within the said area were consumed by the extreme intensity of the combustion.

So after three days, when the coast was clear, you figured out everything got burnt to a crisp?

"If you want to put it that way."

Chief, what caused the fire?

"The matter remains under investigation and scrutiny at this point in time."

You mean you don't know.

"That's pretty much it."

•••

Then it was off to Los Angeles, the home of the televised car chase, where a police chief gave his report.

"The officer observed a reversal of direction contrary to the laws governing traffic flow in and about the State of California and attempted to engage the suspect in question."

So the guy hangs a louie, and the officer tried to pull him over. Then what happened?

"The suspect proceeded at a high rate of speed in an apparent effort to disengage contact with the officer."

You mean he tried to get away.

"In layman's terms, yes. Anyway, as I was saying, we were able to apprehend the suspect without further incident.

You got the guy?

"Uhh, affirmative."

I noticed, Chief Obscurant, that the guy was bleeding profusely. Can you explain?

"The subject responded to his apprehension with physical and verbal actions not conducive to a positive situational outcome."

He hit you and called you names, so you beat the crap out of him?

"We, uhh, responded with the necessary restraint to bring the situation under control."

So you really let him have it?

"I have no further comment on this particular matter at this point in time."

So Chief, where is the guy now?

"The suspect is undergoing emergency surgery at Orange County General for injuries suffered during routine booking at the police station when the subject made an unimpeded descent from the precipice to the base of a walkway designed to allow passage from one floor to another."

He fell down the stairs?

"Correct. Naturally, pending the outcome of the medical treatment, the suspect will be duly processed and incarcerated."

If he lives, you're gonna put him in jail?

"That's what I said."

•••

Even in small communities, the scourge of Official Speak is prevalent. Will's next stop was in Slippery Slope, ND, where the mayor met with the press to discuss an embezzlement case by a city employee.

Mayor Pompousass, have charges been filed?

"Not at this point in time."

You mean not yet? Mayor, can you tell us if your Cousin Dubber, the treasurer, is a prime suspect?

"I can neither confirm nor deny that report at this point in time."

Mayor, will you address reports that you have been implicated in this matter?

"I am extremely distressed that the liberal press has chosen to expound upon unsubstantiated rumor in such a gratuitous manner which is clearly not conducive to the proper operations of this city government."

You mean it's all our fault?

"No comment."

Mayor, don't the Feds have you on tape admitting in Ziggy's Bar and House of Illicit Pleasures that you split the money with Dubber?

"I misquoted myself."

© Tony Bender, 2001

A State by any
Other Name

I thought I would be original this week and discuss the discussion about North Dakota's name change. Then, after exhaustive research, I discovered that every columnist in America, four from Canada and one from Bimini, have already beaten me to it.

But I am, after all, an original son of North Dakota, and who would you rather read—some New York fancy pants like George Will, pontificating on the sacred buffalo grass and amber waves of grain, or me? (SHUT UP! IT WAS A RHETORICAL QUESTION, YOU DISLOYAL PUNK!)

Anyway, I was convinced I had the funniest idea of all—to change our handle to The State Formerly Known as North Dakota. Then I read the Sunday edition of *The (Fargo) Forum* in which editorial page editor Jack Zaleski espoused the very same plan, which proves what many of us have suspected for some time now: Jack and I are geniuses.

But I have some other ideas, the likes of which will no doubt raise my standing as a genius in the state. Fact is, had I received just several hundred thousand more votes in the last gubernatorial election, you would already be seeing signs at the borders: North Dakota, Resident Genius: Bender.

Anyway, getting back to my original subject, which near as I can remember was nuclear fission, I want to assure Jack

Zaleski, whom you may recall from 17 paragraphs back, that even if I assume the title of Resident Genius, I shall see to it that he becomes Vice Genius or Genius Emeritus or something official like that.

Now let us move on to my brilliant plan for North Dakota's name change. A few months back, I decided to change my name to something a little more hip-hop, and I figure if it's good enough for me, it's good enough for my state.

I've narrowed it down to Wu-Tang Dakota or LL Cool North. If we pull that off, we'll change the governor's name to Snoop Doggy Guv, outfit him in baggy jeans and a backwards baseball hat. (Yo, yo, yo! Word to the legislature!)

My backup plan is to name North Dakota "The Real Minnesota" just to throw all those former residents who moved east into a tizzy.

It's not that I have anything against them, but I get tired of these emigres coming back to tell us prairie rubes how superior they are now "dat dey liff in Minny-soda where der's carz as far as da eye can see and chust so much to do while sittin in da traffic cham."

Moofing to Minny-soda kin make you plumb soffistikated.

(At this point I want to assure you that this has nothing to do with my brother, a resident of Red Wing, MN—*where dey make dose fancy schmancy chugs*—just because he didn't have the decency to give my book, *"Loons in the Kitchen,"* which screams Pulitzer, a full five stars when he reviewed it on amazon.com.)

Just in case my Minny-soda Backup Plan doesn't find favor, I have a backup backup plan. This plan is based on the Greater North Dakota Association's apparent assumption that by changing our name we will fool the rest of the country into thinking we're not the coldest state in the lower 48—and we are. It's a statistical fact. (But shhh. Don't tell anyone.)

Here's what we do. We take all the states names, put them in a barrel and let Regis Philbin pull them out to rename the states. If there is a God, Texas will become Rhode Island.

As I have listened to the debate about the name change, I wondered for a moment why former governor Ed Schafer waited until he was out of office before helping lead the charge for a name change. Then, almost as quickly, I realized it is because he is not an idiot.

Now, if my plan, backup plan or backup backup plan fail to find support—*imagine that*—I have a fourth option.

Why not capitalize on the truth about North Dakota? Let's put new slogans on our signs:

- *"Are You Tough Enough For North Dakota?"*
- *"North Dakota: No Pansies Allowed."*

Whatever we do, let's not revive the slogan *"North Dakota. Love It or Leave It."* That one kind of backfired.

I think we should use reverse psychology. Let's do an ad campaign telling everyone to stay away:

- *"North Dakota: We Don't Want You Here."*
- *"North Dakota: We Keep the Riff-Raff Out."*

As contrary as Americans are, they will visit just to spite us.

I am confident that one of these plans will be adopted, and I am likewise confident that I will not get any credit whatsoever. Jack Zaleski will say he thought of it first.

© Tony Bender, 2001

The Campaign
Falters

Writer's note: During the 2000 race for governor in North Dakota, which I came breathtakingly close to winning, losing by just a few hundred thousand votes, the Democratic candidate and then-attorney general Heidi Heitkamp made political fodder out of the escape of murderer Kyle Bell. Political populism is the official sport in North Dakota. Despite my political hectoring, Heidi did contribute two dollars to my campaign, and the eventual winner, Governor John Hoeven sent me a dollar, proving both to be good sports.

Lately, I've received a number of inquiries about my gubernatorial challenge, so I thought I'd update you folks on the state of the campaign.

Frankly, the campaign has been slowed by financial concerns. But on the positive side, Bender loyalists can be assured that I will not be drawn into the mire of political favoritism.

Because in order to return a favor, you have to get one first.

We were briefly excited last month when Wahpeton publisher Jim Hornbeck pledged a "three figure campaign contribution."

But with the price of gas, that dollar didn't go too far. In fact, we ran out of petrol just short of Herreid and were forced to hitchhike back to Ashley aboard a manure spreader.

The irony is not lost on me.

But as they say, "Every clown has a sliver lining." While we were stranded in Herreid, we broke out the Discover card and spread some cheer at the local watering hole. So I'm confident, come November, we're going to carry the Herreid vote and maybe Mound City, too.

Of course, the fact that both communities are across the border in South Dakota does complicate the issue. So we've been trying to get local rock star Mylo Hatzenbuhler, the Strasburg Superstar, to pull some strings and have Strasburg annex Herreid.

But Mylo is playing hardball. He wants a favor or two. The 17 prune kuchens are no problem, but I am not sure exactly how I will convince legislators to make the Holstein the state bird.

Anyway, that's as far as I go. Just because I desperately need a favor and my campaign is in shambles, I'm not going to shamelessly promote Mylo's web site www.farmboymusic.com and encourage folks to purchase his newest album, "All the Cows I've Milked Before," just because the man is a musical prodigy, exemplifying the combined genius of Hank Snow, Ray Conniff and Clarence "Frogman" Henry.

No, I shan't lower myself.

Perhaps the biggest distraction to the campaign has been the lawsuit we recently filed against Herbie's Goat Transport of Danzig.

Maybe you heard about it. Herbie was hauling a bunch of renegade goats to Wishek Livestock (the official livestock auction of the campaign), when one of them escaped through a hatch in the roof of the stock trailer.

Well, there was quite a to-do around these parts because having a sociopath goat roaming the area makes folks as nervous as George W. Bush at a pop quiz.

So we publicized the escape on KQDJ Radio in Jamestown on Wayne Beyers' show, *Stutsman County's Most Wanted Goats.*

Well, inside a month, we were tipped off that the goat was hanging out in Monango where surprisingly he had blended in quite unobtrusively with the locals.

Residents were shocked at the arrest. "You know, he seemed like your average goat," said a neighbor. "He was quiet. Kept to himself. Very polite. Now it gives me chills to think we were living right beside a renegade goat."

Well, this goat hunt came at no small expense to the taxpayers of North Dakota, so we have gone after Herbie for $527— enough to make an intra-lata phone call on U.S. West (which, considering the clarity of the line and the exemplary service, is a real bargain).

Naturally, political opponents have accused me of exploiting this unfortunate goat escape for political gain. Let me say now that despite the fact that a high-profile populist lawsuit on behalf of the beleaguered taxpaying citizens of this glorious state by a candidate might win votes, it remains a coincidence.

© Tony Bender, 2000

Campaign
Update

I've been flooded with letters, e-mails and phone calls wondering about the status of the Bender for Governor campaign. I even received a substantial donation from a 92-year-old man, Herman D. Wildermuth, who lives in California.

While we suspect the money might be PAC money, something we have sworn not to accept (mostly cuz we weren't getting any anyway), our California friend claims he found the money during his daily two mile walks.

One of the coins is French. We can tell because it hates us, never bathes and pretends not to understand English even though it does. We're a little concerned about the implications of foreign contributions. But then, California is already about as foreign as you can get.

I also received a cryptic note from a gentleman wondering "When is it officially dark?" I surmise the question has something to do with a traffic ticket involving the nighttime speed limit of 55. According to intense in-depth research by my staff (me), we have deduced that it is officially dark whenever your local police officer damn well says it is.

Around here, though, it's not the police that intimidate nighttime drivers into slowing down, it's the vast herds of deer intent on grazing blacktop at night.

In fact, the "deer excuse" has eclipsed "The dog ate my homework" as the number one teen excuse in the our area. Whenever a teenager is involved in a one-car accident, they explain it is because, "a deer ran out in front of the car."

They swerved to miss it, lost control, da da da da... And they were only going 35 mph when they rolled seventeen and a half times. Really. This usually happens around 3:45 a.m. because deer, typically, are stumbling home from the party at the same time.

As governor, I intend to lock teenagers and deer in a room until they straighten this whole thing out.

© Tony Bender, 2000

Elmo Dodges Cremation

Everyone has a relative they'd just as soon not have visit. With me, it's Old Uncle Elmo. I've actually changed jobs and moved to avoid a visit.

When I see him at family gatherings, I always lie when he asks me where I live. "I'm homeless, Elmo. I hang around down at the rail yard a lot."

"Really?"

"Yeah. I know every engineer on every train, all of their children and all of their names."

"You can't get a room anywhere?"

"Sure, but no phone, no food, no pets... And I ain't got no cigarettes."

"I didn't know you smoked."

"Forget it, Elmo."

So I was more than a little surprised when the phone rang the other day and it was Elmo on the line.

"How'd you get my number, Elmo?"

"Cousin Gert." (She always was a snitch.) "I figured I'd come-on out to Hettinger for a visit this month. You can pull my finger just like the good old days."

"Uhh, Elmo, now's not a good time. Haven't you heard? The County Commission is cremating poor old folks in Adams

County."

"Ach, can that be? Why do they want to do that to old codgers?"

"I dunno. For being old and broke, I guess. Cremation is cheaper."

"How many they cremate so far?"

"Well, they actually haven't gotten around to cremating anyone yet. Every time an indigent dies, the local undertaker grabs them and refuses to surrender the corpse."

"Boy, that must be something."

"It is. You've got SWAT teams outside with bull horns. But that undertaker fella just barricades himself inside, yelling things like, 'Over my dead body, coppers!'"

"So what does the County Commission think about this?"

"Well, Elmo, that's why now is not a good time. They're getting real itchy to cremate someone. When they see some old lady walking down the street, sneezing from a cold, they start following behind with butane torches. Reminds me of buzzards in the Serengeti."

"No."

"Yes. Old Martha Watson took a tumble across the street the other day, and by the time I got there, she was having a conniption fit cause she was sure if she didn't get up in ten minutes they'd cart her off.

"But you're not indigent, Martha," I said.

"I knew I shouldn't have worn this tattered old coat," she said.

"Sounds like everyone down there is getting a mite skittish."

"Indeed, Uncle Elmo. I couldn't guarantee your safety—not at your age. Now if you come down here and get cremated, how am I gonna explain that to the rest of the family?"

"I see your point, Tony. No sense taking chances. Maybe I'll see you at the next family barbeque. Of course, I'm not sure if anything grilled is going to appeal to me."

© Tony Bender, 1996

Writer's note: A lot of folks got riled up when the Adams County Commission decided that if they were going to have to pay for indigent funerals, they would employ cremation because it was cheaper. The funeral home didn't like it, I'm sure because they wouldn't get paid as much. One old guy came to talk to the commission. "I hear you're going to cremate <u>indignant</u> people," he said. Well, if they had cremated all the indignant people, the population would have been trimmed by a good third.

Once, when a resident at the nursing home died, a man from the crematorium came nearly 200 miles to pick up the body, which had been removed by the local funeral home. They refused to give up the body. It all got pretty silly. I don't think the commission ever actually got anyone cremated, but dad-gum, you gotta give them credit for trying.

The Governor
Saves ND

There are a few things I believe unhesitatingly. I believe Bill Gates is the most powerful man in the world, rivaled only by David Lee Roth. I believe Janet Reno has the hottest legs in the Clinton Administration. I believe baking soda can do just about anything and that we got the recipe from aliens. And I believe North Dakotans have an inferiority complex.

When Clinton suggested that getting rid of North Dakota might make economic sense, the Military Industrial Complex, which assassinated JFK, started the Spanish American War and moved *Murder She Wrote* from Sunday nights, loved the idea. They thought they were going to get to invade some pipsqueak foreign nation. In the biz, they refer to it as "doing a Grenada."

Naturally, Governor Schafer stood up for North Dakota. Because nobody likes to be told he's governor of a state that could be eliminated and never missed. He got on the hotline, the direct line that leads right from the governor's office to a Washington, D.C. Dominos. Luckily, the President was there picking up some takeout. What are the chances?

"Ed who?" the President asked.

"Ed Schafer, governor of the Great State of North Dakota."

"Schafer, hmm? Nope, doesn't ring a bell... "

"My dad's the guy who invented Mr. Bubble."

"Oh yeah. Paula Jones had some weird sort of fetish about the stuff. So what can I do for you, Fred?"

"Mr. President, I was a little upset by your recent remarks suggesting we could do away with North Dakota..."

"Just a joke, Ted. Here at the White House, we know how important North Dakota is. That was just a speechwriter's joke. Heck, what would we do without Mt. Rushmore? "

"Beg your pardon?"

"You know, the hill with George, Teddy, Jefferson and Abe Vigoda carved on it."

"Actually, Mr. President, Mt. Rushmore is not in North Dakota."

"So what do you have in North Dakota?"

"Wheat, sir. We have wheat."

"Oh yeah. Ron Brown used to send me memos about wheat. How does that work again?"

"Well, at the cost of about $90 an acre the farmer plants the seed, fertilizes the land, sprays it for weeds and bugs and watches it hail. In an average year, a good farmer can make back up to $85 an acre."

"So what you're telling me, Ned, is North Dakota is filled with looney farmers where ice falls from the sky every summer."

At this point, Governor Schafer got real indignant. Because the truth hurts.

"Mr. President, do you understand that without North Dakota wheat, your pizza wouldn't have a crust?"

"That seals it, Jed. I'll call the Military Industrial Complex right away and call off the invasion."

That's the little known story of how Governor Schafer saved North Dakota.

Other public officials have suffered similar indignities. To paraphrase Kermit the Frog, it's not easy being from North Dakota. You start living in a state of clinical denial. Which is why, I assume, that one North Dakota politician, tired of listening to senators from the coast bragging about their naval bases, wrangled a U.S. Coast Guard Station for LaMoure.

You've got to admit, that's a good one. Our man cited national defense as the reason for the base. He said it would keep the Finlanders out. In reality, nothing can stop a determined Finn. But in all fairness, not one Russian submarine has ever made it down the Jim River.

Now, military bases across the country are being threatened by budget cutbacks. They're sweatin' it out in Minot and Grand Forks but frankly no one in Washington even knows about the LaMoure Coast Guard Station. Not even the Coast Guard.

Anyway, they're doing a great job in LaMoure. Back in 1982, when a young boy had his little toe nibbled by a passing carp, the Coast Guard jumped into their eight-foot Alumacraft, fired up the 35 horsepower Johnson outboard after just seventeen pulls, went out there and beat that carp to death with an oar. I don't know if you can justify the station based on national security interests, but they're doing a whale of job keeping the carp population down.

Another face-saving political move was the creation of the North Dakota State Forest Service. After all, a guy can listen to those California hot shots talk about their redwood forests just so long. Now let's face it, if North Dakota has a forest, we're doing a pretty dang good job of hiding it. At last count, there were 173 trees in North Dakota. That's down from last year's count because they cut down an old cottonwood on Hettinger's Main Street and a tall gopher on a hill near Gackle was mistakenly counted as a small fir.

So rare are trees in North Dakota, our foresters carry around wallet-sized snapshots of their favorite trees like grandpas fill their billfolds with photos of grandkids.

Sure, we're in denial about trees in North Dakota. But we're trying. And the good news is the tree count could double in 1997. A farmer near Amidon is talking about planting a shelter belt in the spring.

It can be frustrating coming from North Dakota. Rand-

McNally tried to eliminate us from the atlas. To be fair, it was McNally. Rand was against it the whole time.

But personally, I feel good about living in North Dakota where a child can pursue a career in forestry or the Coast Guard. Here the great American dream of only losing $5 an acre on wheat still lives. This is the birthplace of Lawrence Welk and Mr. Bubble. And Mt. Rushmore is located a scant 250 miles south of Mott.

© Tony Bender, 1996

Writer's note: I like Ed Schafer. Shortly after he was elected, he was invited to speak to the North Dakota Newspaper Association Convention, and he used his time to chew us out for being too invasive and downright nosy. I was in the hall grinning at him when he walked out after his speech.

"I'm not sure I should have done that," he said.

I assured him we'd get over it. "Governor you have large cajones," I said. In North Dakota you can say that sort of thing to a governor—at least the precedent has been set.

Technology Issues

Bring back the good old days when we had a telephone company monopoly in America. Sure, they had you over a barrel but at least you knew where you stood.

I boiled over the other night when trying to collect a 10% rebate on long distance calls we'd accumulated over the past year. The deal is, after a year with Sprint you are supposed to get your rebate. For two days I tried to get through to Sprint. They're a phone company—don't they ever answer? All I got was the usual maze—"Press #1 if you wish to spend a whole bunch of money with us. Press #2 if you'd like to remain on hold until your children graduate."

Every time I punched the number for customer service, I'd get cut off. True story. So finally, on Day Two, I figure it out. I press the number indicating I'm a new customer. They answer on the first ring. That really ticks me off. Then the customer service representative explains that I won't be eligible for my discount until December 20. She is unable to explain why that is, but the gist of the conversation is, I'm pretty much shafted.

I scream. I stomp. I wave my arms. The Redhead thinks I'm doing the Macarena. My customer service representative agrees to take up the matter with her supervisor, Mr. Beelzebub. He confirms that I am shafted.

I go ballistic. I threaten to call the PUC, BBB, FBI, CIA, NDEA, ACLU, UB-40 and B.B. King. I've got the *Low Down Cheatin' Scumbag Phone Company Blues.*

Next day, as if to kick me when I'm down, I get a bill from Sprint. I figure it out. I'm paying 18 cents a minute—a far cry from the advertised 10 cents a minute plan. Apparently I didn't read the disclaimer: *Offer good unless customer calls anyone with a vowel in their name.*

Tony Bender
Missing the Phone Monopoly, 1996

Monks and
Goat Sacrifices

Ihate my computer. All of my computers. But it's not just my
computers I hate. I hate all the paraphernalia that goes with
computers—the printers, scanners, software and digital cameras.

Technology is the devil. Or at the very least, a spiteful mis-
tress. Sleek, sexy and ready to turn on you like a wild dog.

It must have been sunspots. Solar flares recently hit an 11-
year high, you know. In one week, two computers, a scanner
and a digital film reader flaked out at my office.

With a newspaper deadline looming, I was forced to call the
local monastery. "Send over fifty scribes and make it snappy.
And go easy on the Benedictines this time!"

The last time I ordered scribes, they sent over a bunch of
deaf bell ringers to take dictation. You can't believe what they
did to the story about chicken plucking. I'm still getting hate

mail from PETA and fan letters from some perv in Billings.

Meanwhile, I called tech support. The final draft of the Venturia Centennial book was on my new iMac. Though I did have a backup, it wasn't the most recent version, and I wasn't ready to give up on a day's work.

After walking through the checklist, tech support advised me to send it in. *Translation:* "All hope is lost and I am about to take all your money."

Still, I wasn't about to give up and finally did manage to get the machine limping along.

Tech support was impressed.

"How'd you do it?"

"Prayer chain, and we sacrificed a goat on the counter. It was kind of messy."

"That's kind of extreme, isn't it? I can't remember the last time we did a goat sacrifice."

"Desperate times call for desperate measures," I said. "Besides, the monks loved it."

That evening, I was forced to wrestle my iBook on line so Dylan, as advised by his television set, could check out "Cartoon Network duck com."

It wasn't easy. I recently hooked up a USB hub which had caused all sorts of consternation. USB is the latest technology which allows you to plug in printers and scanners and such to your computer.

You used to have to do that with old-fashioned SCSI (scuzzy) cables which could get complicated and often didn't work.

Now the system has been streamlined. You can use a simple USB plug to make your computer lock up.

Now, before all the Windows purists start feeling too smug, let me say, we've had our fair share of problems with our Microsoft-driven computers as well. We've killed whole herds of goats trying to solve problems on our circulation computer.

And I really resent the error messages on Windows computers. "YOU HAVE COMMITTED AN ILLEGAL OPERATION!"

An illegal operation? That's a little harsh isn't it? Some days I expect Bill Gates and his Seattle nerds to kick in my door, pull slide rules from their pocket-protectors and start roughing me up.

On the other hand, my Macintosh doesn't come right out and say that I made a mistake. It says to me—out loud, in a Steven Hawking voice—"It's... not... my... fault..."

So you have one computer that acts like Stalin with hemorrhoids and another that sounds like a paranoid flower child.

Here are some other comparative messages I have received.

Mac: "Oops! You may want to rethink that command..."

Windows: "Touch that key again and I'll open up a can of whup-ass on you!"

Mac: "So sorry! The document has failed to print because of a postscript error."

Windows: "Listen turd, I'm not going to print. So what are you going to do about it?"

Mac: "Oh no! I'm feeling faint. Your Finder has quit. You may want to save changes and restart."

Windows: "Look dinkus, I don't want to open that program today. Deal with it."

But better times are coming. Both Apple and Microsoft are coming out with new, more stable operating systems. Mac has OS X and Microsoft has Windows XP.

Now things are going to be just fine and dandy.

They promise.

©Tony Bender, 2001

Too Soon to
Eat the Dog

We were startled when the telephone rang New Year's Day. Fully outfitted in camouflage, I crept low past boarded up windows to answer.

"Eva Braun Memorial Bunker."

"Happy New Year!" said the voice of a friend. "Didn't see you out last night. Wow! What a party!"

"You were out looting?" I asked.

"Looting?"

"Yeah, you know. With Y2K and the end of the world and all that."

"Nah, just your basic New Year's party."

Wasn't he afraid of power outages? Shortages of precious commodities?

"Well, we did run out of beer," he allowed.

Just as I suspected. Anarchy. No doubt there were roving mobs with German accents, torches and pitchforks, forcibly wrestling kuchen and liver sausage from the helpless hands of the unwary.

With the unexpected miracle of phone service, I would have turned on the television to see if it worked had we not chopped it up for kindling just hours before.

So we tuned in the battery powered shortwave hoping to find

a glimmer of civilization. Maybe the BBC. Radio Havana. I'd settle for anything. Then, bursting from the crackly speaker came the familiar strains of Blue Oyster Cult. "Don't Fear the Reaper."

Like that wasn't a sign.

But when the newsman came on, he seemed relaxed. I expected just a hint of terror in his voice. But these guys are professionals. The news was pretty much ho-hum. It looked like Australia had come through the Y2K thing OK, he said. Big deal. How tough can it be to make a kangaroo Y2K compliant?

In the beginning, I didn't take this Y2K thing too seriously. But then all the power companies started assuring us that everything would go just fine. However, it was merely coincidence that they would be fully staffed at midnight. We heard the same assurances from government, hospitals, banks and other critical services.

Well, if there's one thing I've learned, it's when people start assuring you that everything is OK, that's when you have to worry. You see it in the movies all the time. Some guy is lying there, pretty much eviscerated, crimson bubbles spouting from his nostrils with each fading breath, and all sorts of folks are standing around telling him "Everything is going to be OK."

Sure, it's just a scratch.

For the observant, there were signs along the way. In June, our dishwasher went out. Then a few days ago, our garage door opener failed. Coincidence? I think not.

"That's why we cashed in our mutual funds and purchased case lots of Sucrets, which we firmly believe will be the favored currency of the new millennium.

As I pound out this farewell on the typewriter I traded for my computer, a case of Charmin, and a manual can opener, homing pigeons perch nearby ready to carry this last message to any remaining vestiges of civilization. As their reward for a successful mission, they will be served with dumplings.

Then, while The Redhead and Dylan huddle in fear, I plan to stalk into town to loot the grocery store. It's probably pretty well

139

picked over by now, but if I can escape with a jar of salsa and maybe some mandarin oranges, I'll consider my mission a success.

Of course, I may arrive to find everything completely normal.

The power on.

No rioting in the streets.

No long lines begging for a ration of heating oil.

Computers and e-mail working just fine.

No National Guardsmen in the streets.

No alien mother ships transporting specimens to the Planet Zandor.

No Pete Rose in the Hall of Fame.

No horsemen of the Apocalypse.

Maybe we should have waited just one more day before eating the family dog.

© Tony Bender, 1999

Ink in My Veins

This session, some dippy legislator introduced a bill that required stiff penalties for song lyrics that encourage children to commit suicide or lead them to substance abuse. But after impassioned testimony from Scary Spice, and the revelation that the *Beer Barrel Polka* would have to be banned, the measure was narrowly defeated.

Another item under consideration is allowing out-of-state newspapers to be official county papers in North Dakota. That will make it incredibly convenient for readers who will get to subscribe to *Sheepherders Gazette* in Montana to read the county commission proceedings. While we're at it, let's make Billings the capital of ND.

Tony Bender
Stop Them from Legislating, 2000

I Wrote
the Book

I realize now it was an elaborate ruse. In recent years, I heard from readers who suggested I ought to put my best columns into a book.

I would then patiently explain that those four columns would more or less result in a brochure.

But eventually I succumbed to ego and the idea that I, a veritable column-writing wizard, should be published. Now the obsequious fog has lifted, and I clearly see that everyone of those advisors must be in league with my book wholesaler and printer.

It's not that I didn't do a little research about getting published, but I should have realized that when a guy like Stephen King decides to bypass the system and publish a novel on the Internet, something is amiss.

In my research, I came across the story of an agent who finally had gotten an agreement to get his client's book published. He called the author with the news: "It's Random House for $7,500!"

There was a long silence at the other end of the line. Finally the author spoke: "But I couldn't possibly afford that!"

I decided to call another regional author in an effort to learn what mistakes he had made so I could avoid them. He was quick to volunteer the names of the companies that had given him "a good screwing." I'm not an empath, but I swear I detected a hint of bitterness in his voice.

Despite the warning signs along the path of this venture, I slogged onward.

I called the regional buyer of a major chain of bookstores for advice.

"What's the name of the book?" she asked.

"Loons in the Kitchen."

"I like it. But the most important thing is the cover."

"I thought you can't judge a book by its cover."

"People do."

So there you have it from an expert. You *can* judge a book by its cover.

The photo shoot for the cover was a disaster. Loons are very disagreeable birds and they excrete a lot. One of them got stuck behind the refrigerator. We decided that loons should best be photographed in their natural environment. So while you will see loons on the cover of the book, you will not see kitchen appliances.

Needless to say, we have a fair amount invested into a full color cover featuring loons—which are black and white.

I then called the regional book wholesaler who was decidedly not excited about buying my book.

"Look," I said, "I'm sure everyone who calls you thinks he has a great book..."

"100 percent of them."

"And probably, most of them suck," I continued.

"About 80 percent..."

"But mister, if you're not going to do it for me, buy it for the loons who were emotionally scarred during the production of this book."

"I'll take five cases."

I was stunned. "So what sold you? The part about the psycho loons?"

"Nah. I hate loons."

"So you're going to buy this book; even though, there's an 80 percent chance it will suck?"

"Sure. If we only distributed books that didn't suck, we'd be out of business."

Then he explained his terms. "I get a 60 percent discount off the cover price and you pay for shipping."

"That sucks."

"Yup. So what's the price of your book?"

"Five hundred dollars," I told him.

The book will be out in October. There will be full color black and white loons on the cover. It will cost $500 and has an 80 percent chance of sucking.

The smart money is on Stephen King.

© Tony Bender, 2000

Writer's note: Against all odds, Loons in the Kitchen is in its second printing. And the smart money is still on Stephen King.

I Don't Do
Rope Tricks

It all sounded so very glamorous in the beginning. As a full-fledged published author, I would travel the Dakotas to bookstores for promotional book signings.

I would be a charming guest on radio and television shows, and newspapers would be thrilled to publish glowing features and reviews about my book. That's how it was all supposed to work.

Most bookstores placed me at a table near the door with a stack of books and a sign that declared I was a "great story teller," or a "powerful new voice of the Dakotas" except in Fargo where the sign must have read: DANGER! LEPER WITH INFECTIOUS WEEPING SORES, judging from the number of books I signed in the longest two hours of my life.

A shutout was narrowly averted thanks to one man who judged that a stack of five of my books would be "just about right" to level out his couch with the missing leg.

And later, God bless them, a former Ashley dentist and his wife stopped by to purchase a couple books, give me a pocketful of toothbrushes and politely suggested I floss more.

But mostly, people avoided eye contact with me the way city folk avoid panhandlers a week from payday.

One young man, who later identified himself as a D.C.

146

lawyer, occupied me with a twenty-minute conversation about politics before ambling away without buying a book. I felt like I had performed the literary equivalent of a lap dance without getting paid.

I have since instituted a couple rules. First, I will talk to anyone for an extended period of time, but first you must buy a book. Secondly, any Washington lawyers attending my book signings will immediately be pummeled soundly about the face and ears with a Tom Clancy paperback and tossed through the front window.

So grim was the turnout, the bookstore manager gave me a beautiful pen, but having watched legions of game show losers, I recognized it for what it was—a parting gift.

Certainly, the absence of local media coverage had harmed the effort, she opined soothingly. "Yes," I thought. "Won't the folks at *The Forum* be sorry to learn they could have had the scoop on the leprosy outbreak." Instead, they were probably dinking around with an in-depth feature on head lice.

As a newspaper owner myself, I recognize the hypocrisy. As a publisher, I resent anyone trying to get "free advertising." But as an author, I embrace it.

Some writers have a schtick to attract book buyers, one bookstore promotions director advised me. "One local author did rope tricks. It was great! Do you do anything?"

"Well, I can play a passable version of Battle Hymn of the Republic with my armpit," I bragged, "but it's still a little rough around that grapes of wrath part."

I could see I was losing her.

"And I am a leper with infectious weeping sores!"

She said she would get back to me.

But there were some minor moments of glory. In Aberdeen, when I arrived, there was a bona fide line waiting for me. Of course, I had been positioned near the restrooms, so I may not be able to claim everyone in the line as a fan.

The turnout was aided by excellent radio and newspaper cov-

147

erage in which the reviewer, apparently searching for something kind to say, noted that my book had "very good punctuation."

As I settled in, I heard two ladies discussing me. One said to the other, "I glanced at the review this morning, but I can't remember what it said..."

I interjected. "It said that this guy is some sort of literary genius, and your life will have a large, gaping, pitiful void if you fail to buy this book."

"That's not what it said!"

"Well, I might have been paraphrasing a little bit," I admitted.

Still, she bought two books—one for herself and another for her 82-year-old Aunt Myrtle to whom I inscribed, "Baby, I miss your red-hot monkey love. Love and kisses, Tony Bender."

Then another woman stepped up and smiled brightly.

"I hear you do rope tricks," she said.

© Tony Bender, 2001

Columnist
Runs Amok

Writer's note: I suppose every columnist crosses the line once in a while. Or at least, you stretch it far enough that editors and readers alike get a little nervous. Kurt Vonnegut says he goes to the edge because the view is great from there. As a writer, I am always amused by the power we give certain words. Who decides what words are swear words? I wondered. Heck, words are just letters lined up in a particular order, I said in one column. Wow, that got a whole lot of folks worked up. Around the same time, I wrote a spoof questioning the sexual preferences of some notable North Dakotans. Lots of editors squirmed... I was a little surprised because from my perspective, who cares about the sex lives of anyone? It bores me. I was just poking fun in a satirical manner about issues that to my mind, really ought not be issues at all.

I received several messages from worried editors last week concerning the content of recent columns which are published in their papers.

My mother even called about last week's column in which I suggested that all words, including swear words, are created equal. I'm sort of the Abraham Lincoln of swear words. Set them free from the bondage of second class citizenship, I say.

MOM: *"Son, what were you thinking when you put all those vulgarities in your column?"*

ME: "It was a typo, Mom. Those things happen."

MOM: *The same exact typos in 18 newspapers?!"*

149

ME: "I know. What an incredible coincidence. I mean, what are the odds?"

I also received an e-mail (entitled "Yikes!") from *Cavalier Chronicle* Publisher Lynn Schroeder in which he suggested I had "run amok." Lynn said that apparently, judging from the number of canceled subscriptions, I had once enjoyed good readership. "Never, never cross the line again, you filth merchant!" Lynn said. (Actually he said no such thing, but I figure this will play well in Cavalier.)

Lynn also was curious about the reaction back here in McIntosh County. "No real reaction at all," I e-mailed back. "A priest did come in to drop off the weekly devotional and mumbled some Latin and waved his hands a bit. It might have been some sort of exorcism."

Patrick Kellar, the good church-going, God-fearing editor of the *Valley City Times Record*, also left a message for me to call him IMMEDIATELY!

However, by the time I worked up the courage to dial, he had left for the day. *"May I take a message?"* his secretary asked.

"Yes," I responded, "Tell him I think that Tony Bender is the greatest columnist I've ever read! Tell your editor that whatever they're paying Bender, it isn't enough for such insight and eloquence!"

"May I have your name sir?"

"Uh, no," I answered, "I'd like to remain anonymous…"

"I understand completely, sir."

My recent column announcing my bid for the governorship, also caused no small amount of consternation—especially the part where I may or may not have not suggested that several prominent North Dakota public officials are gay.

Now, one of the phone calls sounded a lot like Public Service Commissioner Leo Reinbold, but I can't say for sure and in the interest of accuracy, I won't even suggest it might have been him.

"Let me talk to the editor," the caller said.

"This is he," I answered, "To whom am I speaking?"

"Well, it's not Leo Reinbold, that's for sure!"

"What can I do for you, sir?"

"Hey, what's with saying all those Republicans are gay?"

"First of all, by gay I meant jolly, and second, I included at least one Democrat."

"OK... So why don't Norwegians hunt elephants?

"I don't know..."

"Because the decoys are too heavy! Ha Ha Ha"

"That's a good one, Leo!"

"I told you it's not me!!!"

Non-Leo also warned me that because of the recent reckless nature of my columns, my chances for winning the gubernatorial race were dwindling.

As all political losers say, it's not about winning, it's about bringing forward the issues to the citizens of North Dakota. I say, if we can shed light on the plight of the cuss words, then we have done our job.

I have noted that it is politically in vogue to confess to all past transgressions before desperate political opponents can expose the dirt. That considered, let me now confess, that when I was very young...George W. Bush did a lot of drugs.

At this juncture, I also wish to make an announcement that upon my election, I shall appoint Redd Foxx my Secretary of Nomenclature. Now, my political advisers have railed against this decision—mainly because Redd is dead. ('Lizbeth, he's coming to join you, honey!)

And those aligned against this juggernaut campaign, complain that Redd's appointment is nothing more than a blatant attempt to secure the black vote in North Dakota.

Ha! They are so off base. It is an attempt to secure votes from *dead black comedians* in North Dakota.

© Tony Bender, 1999

The Threat
of Velcro®

Whew! I'm almost afraid to write a word this week. You see, I've been officially threatened by the Velcro® company.

It seems that I printed the word Velcro® without the ® at the end. The ® is known in the fast-paced corporate world as a "thingamajig."

The Velcro® lawyer in charge of thingamajigs is Shari Ann Strasburg®, who will be referred to hereafter by her initials. *SAS* is the *General Counsel* for Velcro®.

You see, that's the highest rank a legal eagle can attain. First there's lawyer, then attorney and finally General Counsel. *SAS* is a four star general.

"We noticed the attached clipping, which unfortunately misuses the registered trademark Velcro®," General SAS writes. "Such an oversight can serve to weaken the identity and value of our Velcro® hook and loop mark."

So thaaat's why the stocks have been plummeting on Wall Street.

She goes on to explain that if I am referring to generic, run of the mill products, they should be called "hook and loop fasteners."

Well, I'm sure glad we've got that straightened out. But I still had a few questions I've penned a letter to General SAS in New

Hampshire. I'm not going to actually mail it since obviously she is a subscriber to this newspaper and I want to save a stamp®.

Dear General SAS,

Boy, is my face red. I can't believe I actually allowed your fine product to be defamed by publishing its name without a thingamajig.

But I'm curious. Did you know that Velcro® with the ® should be pronounced *Velk-roar?* But I guess that's the way you talk in New Hampshire.

By the way, we love your pigs out here. Hampshire Hogs® are raised all over the county. Just curious. Is New Hampshire the *Pig State* or could we possibly lay a stake to the title—with the proper trademark of course?

Anyway, I want you to know that I have been a proud user of hook and loop fasteners for many years now. Unfortunately, I can't seem to tell one brand from another.

Coca-Cola® has a red can, and Pepsi® has a red, white and blue can. And you can tell a Chevrolet® from a Ford® easily enough. Maybe you guys should put hood ornaments on your Velcro®.

I have studied the *Associated Press Stylebook and Libel Manual©* as you have suggested and was aghast to find that misuse of the ® is punishable by caning. Yikes!

Also, while perusing the book, I studied up on the use of the ©, known in legal circles as a *thingamabob*, which you, as a faithful reader of this newspaper, may have seen at the end of this column.

The general gist of it is that newspaper columns are copy-righted and may not be reprinted without permission. I must have missed your call.

Now, unfortunately, you have sent me proof of your possibly illegal act. Frankly, I'm disappointed. I suppose we *could* drag your butt® into court. The problem is I only have a lawyer and he is out-ranked by you, a general.

153

So I'm thinking that we've both learned a valuable legal lesson here. *I* certainly feel chastened. And I will promise to be a proud supporter of Velcro®, truly a leader in the hook and loop fastener market.

Let's call it quits, OK?

Cordially, Tony Bender©.

© Tony Bender, 1994

Writer's note: This column has been published a couple times since it was originally written. Every time it runs, I get a letter from a Velcro® lawyer, but I hardly get threatened anymore. Let me state here unequivocally, I am a big fan of Velcro®. I love Velcro®. I adore it. I am considering leaving my wife for Velcro®. The world needs more Velcro®.

I'll probably still get a letter.

Memo to Rich

M EMO: Rich Tosches

RE: Snide remarks about Wishek

You had to do it, didn't you Rich? You had to get my editor all riled up.

When I first read your column in the *Colorado Springs Gazette,* taking a few jabs at North Dakota and Wishek, I thought they were funny. Example: *"The capital is Bismarck which is German combining the words Bis (Our) and marck (wagons broke down forcing us to live here and eat the horses).*

Even though your column went on to heckle the Wishek Wildlife Club's Buffalo Supper and guys named Adolf, I defended you at the Association of Commerce meeting. "He's jest funnin'," I told them.

But then, after *Wishek Star* Editor Chuck Sterling came to the defense of his community, you had to try to get the last word, didn't you?

So you wrote, *"The city council recently approved the purchase of $6 worth of postage stamps. Narrowly defeated was a bond issue that would have raised enough to get the town clerk a new glue stick."*

Your snide remarks have Chuck, as we say around here,

155

"madder than a mud wasp in a dry gourd."

Let me tell you a little bit about Chuck. He's 6-7, 287 lbs, used to wrestle under the pseudonym Mad Dog Chain Saw Sterling, eats live wolverines for breakfast and once shot a man in Reno just to watch him die. Incidentally, Chuck is so beloved in Colorado he has a town named after him (No, not Chuck, CO.)

I'll concede that by nature, Chuck is a bit of a curmudgeon. But I like to consider him a jolly curmudgeon. Since your smug remarks, however, he's a changed man. He doesn't Hully Gully to his Tito Puente records any more. And even though we tempt him with his favorite pickled turkey gizzards, he just picks at his food.

So like any good publisher, I must come to the defense of my editor and community. Naturally, I do so with trepidation, taking on a big city "lifestyles" (referred to around here as the "sissy section") writer like yourself.

Your recent columns make the assumption your way of life is vastly superior in Colorado Springs. Motto: Only three brutal homicides this week!

Well, as a North-Dakota born, former resident of Colorado (Denver), I must humbly suggest I am more qualified than you to make the comparisons between Wishek and Colorado Springs. (Other motto: "That stench is coming from Pueblo. Really.")

Let's cover just a few issues:

• Population. Yes, there are more people in Colorado Springs than in Wishek which gives you the opportunity to stand in line a lot more. But according to my calculations, at your recent murder rate, by 2007, the population will have declined below that of Mott, ND. (Motto: "Where's our Hoople?")

• Air quality. I moved back to North Dakota because I prefer air in its gaseous form as opposed to the brown chunks floating along the front range.

• Fishing. Every summer for the past 10 years I have driven to Colorado for a weekend of worm drowning (you call it fishing) with my buddies Tom and Bob. Like you noted in a recent column, fishing at Taylor Lake has been dismal. You might try Mirror Lake. It's just a "hoot and a holler" (the official form of measurement in Tin Cup) from Taylor Lake and fishing has consistently been better. Float some Power Bait 2 1/2 feet off the bottom or cast some flies near the rushes of the north end. *Rookie.*

Anyway, tiring of my annual query, "Where are we going to not catch fish this year," my buddies are coming out to North Dakota this June (if they don't get car-jacked along the way) to catch their limit of walleye, perch, northern pike or trout.

Maybe you ought to consider a visit too, Rich. I was thinking we could crown you Big Wienie during Wishek's world-renowned Sauerkraut Day in October. That was the most humane suggestion gleaned from our recent, and admittedly, unscientific poll, "What shall we do with Rich Tosches (rhymes with douches)?"

Other suggestions involved a bass accordion, farm animals, barb wire and udder balm.

We are hoping you'll set aside some time on your schedule to see the real Wishek, ND. We think you'll find the people of Wishek a forgiving sort with a fine sense of humor.

As a measure of our sincerity, we have started a collection at the *Wishek Star* to help fund your visit. After a week we have seven cents, two Juicy Fruit wrappers and what appears to be a chunk of dog feces. Chuck denies it was him.

© Tony Bender, 1999

Another bill from the geniuses in the ND Legislature...
HB1417 would make the media responsible for false information
provided in political advertising. A newspaper could actually be
fined if a candidate's ad is less than truthful—not that that has
ever happened, mind you. One of the bill's sponsors, Rep. Merle
Boucher, got instant feedback from a newspaper in his district.
The Turtle Mountain Star refused to publish his legislative report
that week. It might contain inaccuracies, publisher Roger Bailey
said.

Tony Bender
Odds and Ends, 1997

Family Ways

The higher we drove on the winding road on our way up the 14,000 foot peak of Mt. Evans, the more nervous Grandpa Bender became.

The road is narrow, and when you look down, you can't see the edge of the road, just the bottom of the valley literally miles below.

"Ach, that's high enough," Grandpa said.

"Nope, we're going all the way to the top," I answered.

"But what if we go over the side?"

"Well, Gramps, you've had a long life."

"But what about you?"

"That, Grandpa," I said, "is why *I'm* driving."

Tony Bender
Generations, 1991

The Easy Part

I caught the bride's eye as she walked down the aisle with the groom. At least I think I caught her eye. She stared straight ahead, not wanting to make public the emotions. I bit my lip for the same reason.

I've known her all my life, and I never prepared myself for the idea that she might walk down the aisle with another man. The day the invitation arrived jumbled among bills and junk mail, I was similarly unprepared.

"Was it hard?" the groom asked me before the ceremony.

The wedding's genesis, the trail that led us to the day, was full of trials, sodden with tears. My place in the journey began more than five years ago when my father called. They'd found a tumor.

It's grueling work, watching someone die, and my mother was there for every moment. I visited when I could and tried to mask shock of the cruel changes in my father.

My act was perfect. And he saw right through it.

Jim had witnessed another battle against the damned cancer. He'd lost his wife.

•••

I still remember the phone call from Mom the day she told me about Jim. She'd sounded cheerful on the phone, and before she hung up, she delivered the news in an 'oh, by the way' fashion. I've long been able to see through the Queen of Understatement. I knew she wouldn't have mentioned his name if he wasn't something special.

Turned out, he was.

Jim has padded softly into our lives, careful not to disturb the memory of my father. He didn't need to be so delicate, but the fact that he was, endeared him to us even more. He's had to learn to deal with our bawdy, outrageous, needling family humor.

Two days before the wedding, I called Mom from work. Jim was there. "Uhh Mom, I've been thinking.... Now I'm not real solid on this, so don't get excited, but you know that part in the ceremony where they ask if anyone objects? I've been thinking about objecting because HE'S POLISH!"

Mom relayed the message somberly, and Jim muttered some weak comeback about German-Russians.

I had other concerns like would I have to change my name to Labesky? Would Jim adopt me?

"I'm changing my name," my mother asserted, "so I can disown you!"

Two days after the wedding, I got a call from Mom.

"Help! I've got a man in his underwear on my couch!"

"Not that again."

"Yes. (disgusted) That again."

"Well, does he look good in his underwear?"

"I've seen better," she replied loud enough for Jim to hear.

After she hung up, I thought some more about Jim's question. "Was it hard?"

No, it wasn't hard at all. We've come full circle, and now we all get to start over again

This is the easy part.

© Tony Bender, 1996

Welcome to
the Real World

Mike got the job. I let out a big sigh, and I realized that I had been holding my breath for the month since I'd talked to him.

"I'm going to work at the Federal Building," he had told me, optimistic as Muhammad Ali on fight night. And he told me about the upcoming interview. I thought of all the other disappointments over the years. Most recently there had been the industrial vacuum cleaner with a mind of its own that had escaped Mike's grasp in a department store tryout.

I tried to cushion the blow. "Well, Mike, I hope you get it."

"I will," he assured me. So I had waited for the outcome.

He's come so very far. I remembered back to the night I desperately paged through my Boy Scout book for CPR tips because I wasn't sure Mike would make the night. I had listened to each pitiful breath with relief and suffered waiting for the next.

The operations had been many. The hospital bills overwhelming for a family with six kids. They knew Mike by name at Mayo.

Yet he thrived. He *grinned* through it all, and we were all desperately in love with our brother. But things were much harder for him. Things came slower, and he understood he was special. Brothers and sisters went on to drive cars, date, to get married and have children, and Mike kept plugging away.

163

He had moved 26 miles away from home to be close to the training, counseling and the boring job that supported him. A group home had given way to the independent apartment he shared with another boy. He had come far, but the disappointments along the way outnumbered the victories.

A job in the real world would put Mike on equal footing. But his steps forward seemed to me ridiculously optimistic, like Wile E. Coyote chasing a Roadrunner dream over the cliff. I prayed Mike would not look down and plummet.

But he had been right all along. When I heard the news from Mom, I called.

"So, Mike, what's going on?"

"Oh, nothing much." (Oh, playing it cool, are we?)

"Well, it had just been a while since I've talked to my Brother Mike so I thought I would call," I lied.

He crumbled. "Well I'm going to work at the Federal Building. Gonna make seven bucks an hour."

"Seven bucks an hour!? Mike, that's more than I make!"

He laughed. A big laugh. The laugh of a young man in the real world. And I laughed too.

The work was hard, he said but "I'm going to do it anyway." He would polish government windows and Uncle Sam's floors.

"Mike, I'm sitting here grinning like a big cat," I told him. "You really deserve it. I knew you could do it."

But I couldn't resist being a big brother just one more time. "Mike, now you work really hard and keep this job. You know how hard you worked to get it. And you know you won't have a vacation for a whole year..."

"I know, but I get Saturday and Sunday off, and that's OK."

I pictured the scene Mom had described after his successful trial. He emerged from the sparkling clean elevator hot, tired and complaining (just a little bit) about an aching back.

"Well, Mike," Mom told him, "Welcome to the Real World."

Yes, Mike, welcome to the Real World. Glad you made it.

© Tony Bender, 1993

A Man's
Gotta Eat

A columnist doesn't ask for much. All you need is material.
Traditionally, in-laws have been the Fort Knox of material
for humorists.

Unfortunately—or fortunately, depending on how you look at
it I have great in-laws. It's hard to complain about The
Redhead's father, Gary. Dylan worships him, and the guy fixes
every broken do-dad around my house when they visit, far
beyond the call of duty.

For instance, when Dylan pulled part of the hitch off my util-
ity trailer (which incidentally was built for me by The Redhead's
brother, Brad), Gary chiseled off the old hitch, lying on his back
in the snow, and then, a few weeks later, attached a new one.

My mother-in-law, Marlyn, has stitched us wonderful quilts
and keepsake teddy bears made from my dad's old sports uni-
forms.

See what I mean? Nice, but boring as all get-out.

I watched Ben Stiller in "Meet the Parents" this weekend and
kept thinking that if I had a psycho father-in-law like the one
played by Robert De Niro, I could write a great book about him
and retire. So I'm starting to resent the denial of material which
has led me to reveal the one dirty little secret about my in-laws.
The one thing that really irks me.

165

The thing is, they're health nuts. Well, I don't know how committed Gary is, but Marlyn is, and you know how that goes.

Now, as far as I'm concerned, that's their business. More power to you. Go ahead, eat your granola and your celery sticks. But when it starts affecting my life, well, then a guy's got to make a stand.

The problem arises when we spend a weekend there. They have deprived me of a sacred ritual which I perform at the homes of all friends and relatives.

When I arrive, I shake the appropriate hands, offer the appropriate hugs, dump the suitcases at the door and open the refrigerator to forage for food.

It was a sad day the first time I foraged at the in-laws. "Oh look! Anyone need a carrot stick? How about some delicious tofu? Or how about a nice tall glass of skim milk?"

It was almost un-American, I tell you. No Twinkies, no Spam, no Moon Pies.

So The Redhead and I developed a plan. Before we got to the farmstead, we'd hit the convenience store in Oakes and stock up on beef jerky and other snacks which we would stash in our luggage. And we would phone ahead and offer to supply lunch—a lard pizza made fresh at the local deli.

Sure, I know it sounds like I'm some sort of ingrate, but a guy's gotta eat.

I almost got ratted out the other day by Eric, Locust's (The Redhead's sister) fiance. I was snacking up in the bedroom when the door burst open.

"Whatcha doin'?"

"Nothing," I replied innocently.

"What *is* that smell?"

"Corn Nuts."

"Cripes, they stink. I guess that explains the damp towel under the door," Eric said.

"Well, a guy picks up a few things in college..."

"Gimme some!"

166

So under threat of blackmail, I did.

Now, I don't want to give you the idea that my in-laws are 100 percent fanatical about health food. Legend has it they do keep some goodies around the house; actual chocolate, the story goes. The thing is, they hide it in a wall safe behind the shredded wheat in the upper-most corner cabinet.

And at least once during a long weekend, they will break out a bag of Doritos®. The thing is, I hate Doritos®. So everyone happily munches on Cool Ranch Doritos®, Super Jalapeno Doritos® and Ultra Cheesy Doritos® while I sulk in the other room, the only one in the house without orange fingers.

Finally, after about five years of this discrimination, I complained. "Hey, anyone around here ever hear of plain potato chips?"

The next Christmas I unwrapped box after box of plain potato chips while everyone else got new CD players, sweaters and jewelry. They thought it was pretty funny.

I guess over the years they've made a few allowances for me. But any self-respecting forager will still find pitiful pickings in the fridge.

On the other hand, a few times a year, Marlyn whips up a pan of my favorite pumpkin bars with the cream cheese frosting. She knows it's not good for me. But she knows a man's gotta eat.

© Tony Bender, 2001

Substitute Hugs

I would be gone the better part of three days. Dylan made a big production out of his mourning, but I knew the truth. This would be a chance for him to have his momma all to himself.

The first clue came when I tried to get a goodbye hug. Dylan was all out of hugs, he informed me sadly. "Mom got the last one." The kid is pretty snugly at bedtime and mornings, but in between it's a crap shoot.

So I resigned myself to being hugless. I certainly would have no luck with my little niece, Katherine.

The girl holds a grudge.

Sure enough, when I arrived, carrying my bags into the basement, she took one surprised look from her perch, sniffed, and nose in the air, walked upstairs.

It all started, I think, about three Christmases past, when we had three babies at the celebration. There was Mary, my brother Scott's girl, who is as cute as a button and as indestructible as a bulldozer.

It was Dylan's first Christmas. He had Don King hair and more than a passing resemblance to Chucky.

Curly-haired Katherine's affliction was the curious jerky motion of her head as she looked around with those serious peepers.

"Reminds me of a chicken," I laughed. "Look at that chicken neck!"

She remembered.

At every family gathering since, I have gotten the cold shoulder.

And I have been shameless trying to win her affection. I comment on her beauty, her intelligence and her grace. I was as successful as a troll begging a date with the prom queen.

But on the second day of my visit, Katherine whispered something into her momma's ear.

"Katherine wants to know if she can give you a hug."

"I think that can be arranged," I responded, playing it cool.

Well let me tell you, when I crawled out of bed the next day, Katherine was waiting outside my door with a morning hug.

She's a marvelous talent, this girl. She romped and she strutted, always with a glance back to see just how impressed I was.

She showed me how she could write her name. "Wow," I said, "There aren't many three-year-olds who can write their name!"

"I'm four," she corrected me in that serious Katherine way.

Nevertheless, I assured her it was quite a feat. I carefully folded the scrawling into my wallet. So pleased was she, that she wrote her name again for me.

During the day, when I was at meetings, she asked when Uncle Tony would be back, my sister reported. When I tinkered under the hood of my vehicle, she watched with admiration from the front door.

I was always greeted with a hug upon my return.

"Katherine, you give the best hugs," I said. "Sometimes Dylan runs out of hugs; does that ever happen to you?"

Katherine assured me she always had an adequate supply.

Sunday, I was sent on my way with a breakfast of eggs and sausage, coloring book art and a great big hug for the road.

At home my boy was pretty spunky after a weekend of serious spoiling by his momma.

169

"Hey Dad, Why did the chicken cross the road?"

"I dunno, Dylan."

"Because he was a glock!!!"

"A GLOCK?!"

"YEAH!"

I laughed so hard I almost fell down. My boy tells the best jokes.

I got a hug, too.

© Tony Bender, 2000

He Hugged Me

"Shall we leave some flowers at your father's grave when we go by?" she asked me.

I bit my lip and stared straight ahead at the Interstate, the yellow lines clipping by like time itself.

I don't revisit my sorrow easily. I take miles of detours to avoid reopening the wound.

After a moment, I nodded—I nodded, because I could not speak—and I glanced out of the corner of my eye to see if she had noticed my pain. She had, but she pretended not to.

My father would have loved her and she him. Sometimes I imagine them meeting. He would be shy. She would be beautiful, smart and classy. And they would both be charmed.

Dylan, the one man commotion machine, would make him laugh. India would sit snug on his lap and he would melt.

171

We took turns keeping vigil by his bed those final days. The hours were long. He could no longer speak, and he drifted in and out of consciousness.

The last day I sat with him—in silence mostly—and when he slept, I read a newspaper. Sometimes I could feel his eyes and I would lower the pages and he would be looking at me, making sure I was there. Making sure that someone was there and that he was not alone.

It has been eight years, but I still can hear the rattle in his chest of the desperate breaths.

Perhaps, to be as strong as he was, is not a gift, for dying is such a hard business and it is better, I think, for it to go quickly.

I had to leave at five—Julie and I were dating then—and Mom was cooking dinner. We had decided, as a family, to go on living, even as my father lay dying.

It is our way. We know no other.

I asked the nurse if...if...

I asked her if my father would live two hours until my mother could resume the vigil.

"There's time," she said, and she had seen death hundreds of times. "It will be a while."

I did not know how to feel. Relief that my father was not ready to go? Or sadness that his suffering must continue?

I went to my father and told him I loved him, and I looked into his grey-blue eyes and I kissed him on the forehead. It was something I had never done. We do not kiss much in our family. It is not our way. But I know that if he had had the strength, my father would have hugged me then.

Our eyes did not break their lock until I walked behind the curtain.

•••

We were almost finished eating when the phone rang. My mother leapt to answer while I bowed my head, staring at my plate, knowing the message.

Pastor Jeff had been with him at the end. They had prayed the Lord's Prayer and then my father was gone.

At least he had not been alone, I thought, waves of guilt washing over me for not being there.

I wrestled with that guilt for years and always it pinned me, helpless, to the floor.

•••

I was dead tired the night he came to me. The hours, the grind of the project, had been a terrible strain. The hours of sleep had been few.

I met him in my dream, and like a father comforts his son with a skinned knee, he comforted me. He did not speak; still he told me he was fine, happy and at peace. And he told me it was time to bury my guilt.

The experts will tell you that a dream is nothing more than neurons and nerves and electricity and chemical reactions, but I do not believe for a moment it is only that. Who is to say a father cannot reach across dimensions to console a child? Of this, I am sure, the angels would approve.

It's better now, and each time I wrestle anew with my regrets, I am comforted by the dream. I am comforted again by my father, who reached across time to do what he could not do in his final hours.

He hugged me.

© Tony Bender, 2001

Writer's note: I got this e-mail after the column came out:

"I worked in Hospice a few years ago, and I just wanted to share something with you that I learned while working there. I didn't know your Dad but my guess is he was a "protector" of the family. Many families experienced what yours did about not being at your loved ones side while they died. I witnessed this many times. One thing our grief counselor and myself (I'm a social worker) liked to share with families is that it sometimes appeared to us and others that the person dying has some control as to the "moment "of death. It seemed like the "family protector" liked to "slip away" when families took breaks from the bedside to go run an errand, have a bite to eat, etc. It seemed to be the dying person's choice to do so. They wanted to "protect" their families one last time. Maybe if you can look at your Dad's dying while you weren't there in this light, it will ease your guilt. You had been with him, said your goodbyes, and he knew that. Please don't torture yourself with guilt of not being there in the moment of death."

Kathy Feil
Mandan, ND

And I wrote back:

Thanks for the kind words. It did seem that my dad did pick the time. They finished praying and it was over. When my wife read the column, she cried. "I always felt guilty that your mother was cooking for me when your dad died," she said.

I'll share this message with her, and I'm sure it will be a comfort to her as it is to me. Mom will get a copy, too. Though we never discussed it, I'm sure she felt some guilt, too.

It took me eight years to write about that guilt, but as I said, "It's better now." I don't suppose we ever really stop mourning our losses. Certainly it is harder when they die so young.

When I took the flowers to the grave Memorial Day weekend, I set six-month-old India beside me as Dylan and Julie walked, to give me a few moments. Then Dylan came to me and said, "Dad, I'm sorry that you're sad that your father died." I gave him a crushing hug.

Dad would have loved him.

Seasons

I reflected a bit on this journey we call life. As carefully as we plan, we don't have the road map. The key, I think, is enjoying the detours and the back roads and the quiet country lanes. And we need to remember we're not always driving. More often than we care to admit, we're in the passenger seat.

Tony Bender
No Road Map, 1996

Moments in
the Season

I would have missed it. I didn't see the young deer in the ditch
as we drove by. But The Redhead did, and she knew something was wrong.

The road was too well traveled. Morning's light reflected
painfully off a hardened snow blanket. Deer do not bed down in
an exposed ditch in broad daylight.

I turned the vehicle around and spotted the attentive ears.
Dylan cooed softly in his car seat. The jolt of freezing air sought
refuge inside when I opened the door.

Twenty-two below. The snow crunched and broke the still-
ness of the moment. The deer turned his head in alarm. But he
didn't get up. When I was within 10 feet he tried, but his hind
legs hung lifeless and bloodied behind him. The animal had been
hit by a passing vehicle. I trudged back to the Explorer to get a

pistol. A helluva beginning to a Christmas holiday.

• • •

Mom talked to one of Mike's supervisors at the Adjustment Training Center. How many wouldn't be going home for Christmas this year? she wondered.

His eyes flashed. "They should all be home for Christmas. This place should be empty!"

She understood his anger. Families still tuck their disabled away. Hidden like a wart on the face they present to the world. For us it had been different. Mike has been the most constant source of honesty and joy in our lives.

The supervisor related a phone call he'd received from Daryl's sister who lives 25 miles to the west.

"What does Daryl need for Christmas?" she asked

"DARYL NEEDS TO COME HOME FOR CHRISTMAS!"

Silence.

• • •

I unzipped the case and loaded the pistol. My hand nearly froze to the metal as I walked back to the deer's final minute.

A seventies-something pickup had stopped beside the deer. Dented bumpers had herded a thousand cattle.

Bales overflowed from the faded gold box.

Twine dangled from a mirror.

The driver wore brown coveralls and a cap with ear flaps. Sensible clothing for the bitter day. Only a reddening nose and two eyes were visible above a coal-black beard.

He saw the pistol in my hand and he nodded. His young son waited in the passenger side, a few steps from the fallen animal. I walked closer. It wouldn't be well to miss. This time the deer just waited. I extended my arm and aimed.

• • •

"Save the tags, Mike, " Mom admonished. Mike opens gifts so fast he sometimes forgets to see who they are from.

I quizzed him. "Who gave you the model?" (I did.)

Mike wilted a little under big brother's interrogation. He did-

178

n't know. But he got my point.

Dylan was one of three babies this Christmas. He fussed when Mary pulled his hair, but he was content when Katherine offered a finger for the teething boy to chew on.

Watching all the children, I reminisced about those Christmases at the farm. We were the kids then. Somehow, I could never imagine those celebrations at the farm ending. But Grandma and Grandpa Spilloway are gone now.

Sherry made Grandma's carmel corn and it was perfect. The mantle has been passed. The tradition flourishes.

Our five-month-old son met Great-Grandma Kane for the first time, and we snapped pictures of Great-Grandma Hanson bouncing him on her knee.

The best gift of all to Dylan on his first Christmas was a handmade brown plaid teddy bear constructed from his Grandpa Gary's coat. Grandma Marlyn made it. The Redhead got one, too. Made from a white fur coat she'd worn as a child.

•••

The safety refused to budge in icy air. And I wasn't about to start pounding on a loaded pistol. I would have to warm it up or retrieve another gun. The deer waited gracefully, with dignity.

The man stopped me. He reached under his son's seat and produced a revolver. The first shot produced no reaction but I saw blood pulsing with each fading heartbeat from the animal's neck. A second shot stilled the animal.

Our eyes met for a moment and then I headed back to my family. "I suppose someone should call the sheriff," he said, his words shattering the dead calm of the late dawn. Then he paused and glanced at my license plate. "But you're not from around here."

I shook my head.

I turned the vehicle around at the nearest intersection and I passed the deer on our way home.

We drove on in respectful silence.

© Tony Bender, 1996

The Magic
Returns

Writer's note: The following column was written in 1992. When I was approached by Dakota Radio Information Service to do a Christmas reading in 2000, I resurrected this column. DRIS is a free radio service provided by the North Dakota State Library for print impaired and learning disabled people.

I saw the Christmas ribbons and paper on store shelves in October this year. October, November, December—that means we spend three months anticipating one day. Can anything live up to that kind of build-up? Most often the answer is no.

But as children, we see Christmas through innocent eyes, and the day is more glorious than we could have imagined. Then we get older and we lose the wonder. We see too many Santas and we miss the message of the season. Our vision fails us. December 25 becomes an anti-climax.

It reminds me of the movie promotions we see and read. We start to believe the perfect movie has been made. But when we leave the theatre, we are disappointed. Our expectations were too high.

Most holidays are like that. And all too often, Christmas doesn't live up to our expectations. But once in a while, the magic returns. It happens when you least expect it—because that is the way magic works.

For me, the magic came in the gloomiest of winters. I was living in Denver, trying to make it in the dog-eat-dog world of big city radio.

I was flying high through the summer, working prime-time hours and the money was good. But as autumn approached, things changed as they do in that madcap world. Promises were broken, my hours were cut and I took another job to make ends meet.

So there I was...radio stardom had been ripped from me and I ended up stocking shoes at K-Mart for minimum wage.

Finally, when my radio hours had been slashed again and more promises broken, I walked away from what had been the best job I'd ever had.

The next day, I got fired from K-Mart. You know you're a failure when you can't hold a job as a stock boy with K-Mart.

Christmas was just days away; I envied the smiling faces nearly buried under packages. I could see families walking hand in hand. Children lagged behind their parents as they watched the blinking lights on the trees. They dawdled in front of store windows filled with toys as I must have done once before the magic slipped away.

I wanted to be home so badly the pain became physical. But home was 700 miles away.

It wasn't the prudent financial move, but my heart was aching more than my wallet, so I packed my bags.

I didn't call to tell them I'd be coming. A surprise was the only gift I could offer that year. Maybe I didn't want to tell Mom and Dad what was happening in my life. Just as they had protected me from unpleasant realities as a child, I wanted to protect them. For they would surely worry.

As I drove through the night, my mind was consumed with the task of explaining my failures. I was going home as a defeated soldier.

But you know, that didn't really matter because the most

important thing was that I was going home.

Home.

Home. I kept repeating the word in my mind as I drove desolate highways.

It was morning when I arrived with an empty gas tank and over-extended credit cards. The Dakota winter had left ice crystals in the trees, and the snow squeaked under my feet as I walked to the front door. I was so eager, I wanted to run. But I didn't.

In my mind, I can still see my hand on the doorknob. I'm sure I was holding my breath. The door opened and creaked once to announce my arrival and to welcome me home.

My youngest brother, Mike, looked up and for a moment his face registered the surprise.

I never completed another step. He sprinted across the kitchen shouting, "Tony, you're home!" He gave me his best bear hug and suddenly in that moment everything was all right.

I realized that holiday weekend that my setbacks were only steps to new victories. I was home and it gave me strength.

Maybe we need to fall once in a while to really comprehend what it means to stand. Would success mean anything if we did not know failure? And perhaps we need to leave home to truly understand how precious it is to return.

My wish for you all is that you too may someday have a Christmas like that. A homecoming like that. But don't expect it. The magic becomes elusive when we look for it.

Magic just happens.

Magic surprises us.

As for me, I don't know if I will ever experience again what I did that day. But every Christmas, I remember.

And the magic returns.

© Tony Bender, 1992

Resolve

I remember watching the fireworks explode from a barge in the calm channel waters off the shores of Juneau, Alaska.

Back home on the prairies flattened by a million buffalo, the rockets seem to rise to the stars. But against the Alaskan mountain backdrop, the rockets fell pitifully short of the peaks. But there, the booms and showers of sparks were ethereal.

The docked USS Juneau was packed with cheering rowdy servicemen. Our boys.

Foreign cruise ships were ablaze with lights and their bands' refrains echoed across to Douglas Island where I watched from the darkened ground that was once Russian.

I thought about my family in the lower forty-eight and of the country that had ventured into this magnificent wilderness of whales, eagles and bears.

With my eyes to the sky and chin up, I watched with new-found wonder—as I must have on my first Independence Day. I stood a little taller. And I remembered that I am an American.

Tony Bender
I am an American, 1993

We Shall Lead

It rained the Friday after the worst terrorist attack ever. It was tears that fell from the sky as a great nation wept, as the terrorist cowards burrowed deep in their hell holes.

The difference between America and Americans and those who seek to bury her has never been clearer. Assassins snipe from the darkness at those who seek to stand in the light. Terrorists soil and litter the landscape, and America will do what it has always sought to do—clean up the mess.

America has been tested and the test has just begun. But America has been tested before by a Civil War that could have torn us apart. But it didn't. We have seen dark days of The Depression. We weathered Pearl Harbor. The Cuban Missile Crisis. The death of Kennedy. Martin Luther King. And another Kennedy.

Each time we were rocked—not because we are weak but because we are a nation of compassion. And when you care, when you wear your heart on your sleeve, as Americans do, your heart can be bruised. Those with black hearts, with no conscience, can never understand. They view our compassion as weakness when it is a great strength.

We may have wondered if we still had it in us to weather the storms. Certainly, terrorists and others who stand against us

185

have wondered. Now they shall see.

America, once complacent, is complacent no more. Americans willing to turn the other cheek so many times before will not do it this time.

Because we are a nation whose leaders change with each election, a nation that bickers and points fingers at our brothers sometimes, the illusion is that we can be easily brought down, that we will crumble when the going gets tough.

But heart is difficult to measure. Just as we do not understand hatred so dark, it drives men to fly plane loads of innocents into tall buildings filled with more innocents. They cannot understand our heart. Our resolve.

We shall need all the resolve past generations have shown and perhaps more.

We must be resolute.

We must be smart.

We must be patient.

Rooting out cowards who shrink from the light is never easy. Like a thief in the night who stole our serenity, our enemy remains faceless. Eventually, the truth will be known. But for now, we must find every terrorist, every rat in the sewer, and we must make them accountable. Our cause is just.

Even people who have stood against us in the past stand with us now. Even in Lebanon, Palestinians wept for America. In Iran, they wept. The Star Spangled Banner rang across the yard at Buckingham Palace. The French gave money to American tourists—donations to be brought back to help heal the terrible wounds.

We have felt alone, we Americans, for so very long, as we have wrestled against those who have no place in this world. But we are not alone.

Still, it will not be easy. This fight will be difficult and drawn out. We will be shaken again. But the fight must be fought.

War has been declared on us and we have no choice. We must defend our people.

186

But we must never lose sight of what the fight is all about. In the hours after the World Trade Center towers fell, after the Pentagon had been set ablaze, some leaders suggested our civil liberties will need to be compromised to fight terrorism.

We must not allow it. We can allow inconvenience. We can allow more stringent security. We can beef up intelligence. But if we set aside our Constitution and Bill of Rights, if we surrender liberty to win this battle, we will have surrendered the very thing we seek to preserve.

And we cannot forget that all Americans, regardless of heritage, have been wounded. We must guard against the prejudices that stained us when Japanese Americans were incarcerated during WWII. America is white and black and brown and red and yellow. But most of all, America is red, white and blue.

We must take great care not to allow the use of this tragic event to further unrelated agendas. This fight is not about prayer in the school or Roe vs. Wade. This is not punishment from God. My God and your God has nothing to do with such things so far removed from the divine.

It was commonly said that America would change after September 11, 2001. Things have changed. We have lost our innocence.

But we must not lose confidence. We must not misplace resolve. We must treasure our liberty.

I believe things can and will change for the better. America is at a crossroads. The road ahead is not to be feared. We should embrace it. There is opportunity here to rid the world of the beasts that taint it. It will take time. We have time. It will take heart. We have miles and miles of heart.

We can be greater than we have ever been. We are Americans, citizens of a world that looks to us now to lead.

We will not cower.

We will weep for a time.

And then we will lead.

© Tony Bender, 2001

Writer's note: September 11 was my 43rd birthday. I was driving 10 month-old India and five-year-old Dylan to daycare when I heard the news on KFYR radio. Dylan chattered happily as I strained to listen. I didn't have the heart to quiet him.

Tuesday is the day we put out the Ashley Tribune. Even on days passenger planes do not slam into national landmarks, it is a stressful day. Adding to the confusion was my scheduled appearance early the next morning in Wahpeton. I was to be the keynote speaker for the United Way fundraiser. From there, Julie and I would fly out to Milwaukee for the National Newspaper Association Convention. The convention was cancelled.

I had planned a humorous speech but after hearing the tragic news, nothing—absolutely nothing—was funny. I hoped they would call it off because I did not believe I could think, let alone speak. But the show would go on, Jim Hornbeck, publisher of the Wahpeton Daily News and United Way chairman told me.

We wrestled with our presentation. Did we dare even attempt humor after such a grave event? We decided to try. But that night in an elegant hotel suite, I tossed and turned to the heartbreaking news on CNN. I wasn't sure I could speak in the morning. To make matters worse, there were rumors of gas shortages and inflated prices. Cars lined up 50 deep at stations in Wahpeton at 10:30 p.m.

"I won't be part of it," I told Julie. "I will not be part of the panic." But I worried. Being away from our children at their grandparents' home near Verona was excruciating. I did not know if we would even have gas to get back to them.

At 1:30 a.m., I was up for aspirin to relieve a rare tension headache. By 4:45 a.m., after a sleepless night, I went for a walk along deserted streets in search of some peace, some meaning to all of this.

By the time we left for the 7:30 a.m. event, I was beside myself with anxiety. But I could hear laughter when I walked into the room, and it gave me hope. I guess it takes more than a dire crises to keep Americans from laughing. God bless 'em. Jim was funny, and I did OK, and then we were off to Verona to hug the kids.

I was working on this book on Saturday and Julie and India were napping, when Dylan came into my office. "Dad, can we go to the playground?" he asked.

It was a good idea. We romped together, and for a few minutes, we forgot about the terrible problems in the world. I watched him run sprints on the football field, and I did not stop him when he ran through the sprinklers, though his mother would be unhappy with us both.

I could not help but worry, as all fathers do. I wondered what the future would hold for him, and I feared he would one day have to fight.

Perhaps the fight will be won by then. I shall pray for victory. We require it.

I require it.

And I want my birthday back.

Photo by Throndset Sudios, Bismarck, ND

About the Author

Long recognized as one of the finest writers in the Dakotas, Tony Bender gained national recognition in 2001 when he was awarded a first place prize for humor writing by the National Newspaper Association for his piece entitled, "The Redhead's Tractor," which is contained in his first collection of writing, *Loons in the Kitchen.*

While acclaimed for his humor writing, Bender's ability to present more serious, heart-warming and introspective aspects of life on the Great Plains also helped him win seven first place newspaper association awards for his column in the '90s.

"He's one of those rare writers capable of deeply touching the full spectrum of human emotions," Patrick Kellar, publisher of the News Examiner, Connersville, IN, said.

Bender began publishing his weekly syndicated column, "*That's Life,*" in 1991, writing for his hometown paper, the *Brown County News* in Frederick, SD. That very first year, Bender scored a first place award for his column in the South Dakota Newspaper Association's annual contest.

The column title was inspired by the Frank Sinatra song.

"*I've been a puppet, a pauper, a pirate, a poet, a pawn and a king,*" the lyrics go.

"*I've been up and down and over and out and I know one thing,*

"*Each time I find myself flat on my face,*

"*I pick myself up and get back in the race...*"

The column has grown in popularity over the years and is now published in a score of Dakota newspapers, read weekly by an estimated 65,000 people.

Born in 1958 in Ashley, ND, Bender grew up in Frederick, a tiny community on the North Dakota-South Dakota border, 26 miles north of Aberdeen, SD. That community with a population of 400 provided Bender with a "Tom Sawyer existence" that surfaces in his writing as he tells the tales of the characters he grew to love.

Because most youths of his age were busy on the farm, Bender found friendship with the colorful retired old men who haunted the benches on Main Street. "It was an idyllic boyhood," Bender remembers. "I think it gave me a perspective and an appreciation for older folks. There's a nobility that can develop with the years," he says.

After a year of journalism at South Dakota State University in Brookings, SD, Bender, in 1977, opted for hands-on experience and embarked on a radio career including stops at KSDN and

KKAA in Aberdeen and KQDJ in Jamestown, ND.

In 1983, Bender moved to Denver where he worked at legendary radio stations KHOW and KIMN.

His sense of adventure took him to Juneau, AK in 1986, where he starred at KTKU with his unique morning show featuring alter-egos like obnoxious newsman Irving R. Osgood and the unscrupulous Rev. Billy Joe Jim-Bob. In 1988, Bender was awarded the *"Goldie,"* a top honor from the Alaska Radio and Television Association, for his accomplishments at KTKU.

In 1989, Bender accepted a morning drive position at WBPR in Myrtle Beach, SC. Shortly after his arrival, Hurricane Hugo struck. While all other broadcast stations evacuated, Bender and his newsman elected to stay to broadcast to the many listeners who had not been able to evacuate in time. As the only station on the air for hundreds of miles delivering crucial information, the effort was widely applauded by South Carolina officials and citizens.

In 1990, Bender returned to North Dakota to be closer to his family, accepting a position as news director at KYYY, Bismarck. In 1991, he took a position as a reporter at the *Williston Daily Herald.* Six months later he was offered the publishership of the floundering *Adams County Record* in Hettinger, ND.

The switch from radio to newspaper was not at all unplanned. Bender says he planned to do radio until he got "too old to be cool on the airwaves." Then he would write. But he's still cool, he claims.

Bender sparked a resurgence in the *Adams County Record* leading it to two *General Excellence Awards*, the highest honor from the North Dakota Newspaper Association. He served as executive news director for the parent company, Dickson Media, until 1997.

Bender did not completely abandon his radio roots in Hettinger. He joined KNDC morning show host Al McIntyre, shark lawyer Tom Secrest and token liberal, Walter Jacobs, New England, for a radio show that was occasionally controversial and almost always entertaining. Where did Bender fit in? "I was the voice of reason," he says.

Bender was presented the first-ever *North Dakota Newspaper Association First Amendment Award* in 2000 for his continuing fight for the public's right to know what their governments are doing. He has championed open meetings through the NDNA Legislative Affairs Committee. "I think government works better under a spotlight rather than in the shadows," he has said.

In 2000, Bender was elected to the NDNA board of directors.

Journalism in small North Dakota newspapers requires many hats be worn. Bender has worn the hats well, judging from top honors received for reporting, sports journalism, photography, advertising, community promotion and design. Bender led the *Ashley Tribune* to NDNA Sweepstakes Awards in 2000 and 2001. He is a two-time winner of the *North Dakota Heritage Writing Contest*. His writing has been published in *North Dakota Outdoors*, *The National Newspaper Association's Publishers Auxiliary*, *The Journal of Indian Wars* and newspapers in many states.

Bender compiled more than fifty of his columns into *Loons in the Kitchen* in 2000. The effort was praised by readers and critics, establishing Bender as a best selling regional author. *Loons* is in its second printing.

"What he's got is a blisteringly funny sense of humor that sometimes teeters on the edge of respectability... (And) it'll take a tough reader not to cry over such pages as *A Mother's Tears* or *Laughter Stolen* or *Dreams For Sale*," Lauren Donovan, *Bismarck Tribune*, said. "Models of human interest reporting and commentary by a gentle man and a devoted journalist," wrote Robert Armstrong, *Minneapolis Star-Tribune*.

Bender and his wife, Julie, have two children, Dylan and India. The couple owns Redhead Publishing, which includes *The Wishek Star* and *Ashley Tribune*. The company publishes niche publications including *Mighty Mac Hunting & Fishing Guide* and *Spring and Fall Ag Outlook*.

To order more copies...

The Great and Mighty Da-Da is available at finer bookstores and we encourage support of those bookstores and book outlets.

The Great and Mighty Da-Da and Loons in the Kitchen are also available online at amazon.com.

Signed copies of The Great and Mighty Da-Da and Loons in the Kitchen are available by sending $21.95 for each book (includes tax, handling and mailing) to Redhead Publishing, P.O. 178, Ashley, ND, 58413

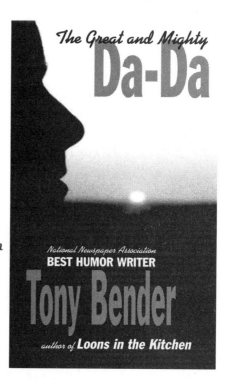

Order Tony's first book!

If you like Tony Bender, you'll love *Loons in the Kitchen!* It includes *The Redhead's Tractor,* the story that won the 2001 National Newspaper Association First Prize!

Loons in the Kitchen and *The Great and Mighty Da-Da,* are also available online at amazon.com. Signed copies of *The Great and Mighty Da-Da* and *Loons in the Kitchen* are available by sending $21.95 for each book (includes tax, handling and mailing) to Redhead Publishing, P.O. 178, Ashley, ND, 58413

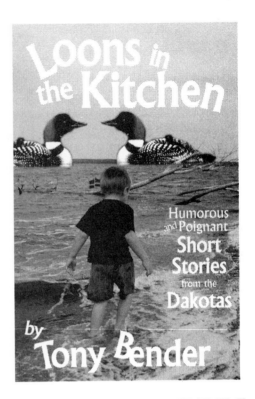